Chaos Unleashed
Stories of Discordian Absurdity
By Ismael S. Rodriguez Jr.

Table of Contents

Dedicated to my fellow creatives who have given me support and
inspiration

Ismael S. Rodriguez Jr. 365 Northwest 43rd Court Oakland Park, FL 33309

https://thebulletproofpoet1.godaddysites.com/

Chaos Unleashed: Stories of Zen and Absurdity/ Ismael S. Rodriguez Jr.

1st Edition

The Chaos Coordinator

The Chaos Coordinator was his name, or at least the name he gave himself. He was a Zen Discordian, a rare and curious breed of mystic who followed both Zen and Discordianism, the philosophies of emptiness and chaos. He was also a teacher, a storyteller, and a trickster. He had traveled the world, seeking paradoxes, absurdities, contradictions. He had learned from many masters, sages, fools. He had found a unique way, a playful way, a chaotic way.

He had found the Discordian Parables.

The Discordian Parables were stories that illustrated the principles of Discordianism, the teachings of Eris, the goddess of chaos. They were also stories that challenged the assumptions of Zen, the doctrines of Buddhism, and the path of enlightenment. They were stories that made no sense, that had no point, that were full of nonsense.

They were stories that revealed the truth.

The Chaos Coordinator decided to share his stories, his wisdom, his humor. He wanted to help others, to teach others, to inspire others. He wanted to spread Discordianism, to create Zen Discordians, to awaken chaos.

He wanted to tell his stories.

He wandered the land, meeting people from all walks of life, telling stories that suited their situations, performing tricks that amazed them or annoyed them. He encountered many situations, many questions, many opportunities. He used his skills, his humor, his magic. He created confusion, laughter, wonder.

He created chaos.

He met a monk who was meditating under a tree,

a farmer who was plowing his field,

a soldier who was marching to war,

a merchant who was selling his goods,

a child who was playing with a ball.

He told them his parables: he told the monk the parable of the hot dog vendor

who enlightened Eris by asking her if she wanted everything on her hot dog,

he told the farmer the parable of the golden apple that caused the Trojan War by being inscribed with the words: "To the Fairest",

he told the soldier the parable of the five-sided Pentagon that became a

four-sided Square by being hit by a plane on 9/11,

he told the merchant the parable of the counterfeit money that was worth more than real money by being accepted as legal tender in some countries,

he told the child the parable of the black and white cat that was both alive and dead by being placed in a box with a radioactive device and a poison.

He taught them his lessons:

he taught the monk to question his meditation and realize that he was not separate from Eris or anything else,

he taught the farmer to appreciate his chaos and realize that he was part of a larger and more complex system than he could imagine,

he taught the soldier to laugh at his war and realize that he was fighting for nothing but illusions and lies,

he taught the merchant to value his absurdity and realize that he was trading for nothing but symbols and numbers,

he taught the child to play with his paradox and realize that he was living in a world where anything could happen and nothing could be certain.

He taught them Discordianism.

He told them his stories, and they listened. Some of them were amused by his stories, some of them were confused by his stories, some of them were angry at his stories. Some of them understood what he was trying to say, some of them misunderstood what he was trying to say, some of them ignored what he was trying to say. Some of them followed him and became his disciples, some of them left him and went their own ways, some of them tried to kill him or capture him.

He didn't care. He just kept telling his stories.

The Cosmic Jester

It was a normal day in the city, until a strange portal opened in the sky. Out of it emerged a bizarre creature, wearing a colorful outfit and a jester's hat. It had a human-like body, but with purple skin, yellow eyes, and a wide grin. It looked around with curiosity and mischief, and then flew down to the streets.

The creature, who called itself the Cosmic Jester, began to cause chaos wherever it went. It used its powers to alter reality, creating illusions, transformations, and paradoxes. It turned cars into animals, buildings into candy, and people into puppets. It made gravity reverse, time loop, and logic fail. It laughed maniacally as it watched the confusion and panic of the people.

The Cosmic Jester had no malice or evil intent. It was simply bored and curious, and wanted to have some fun. It did not understand the consequences of its actions, or the feelings of the people it affected. It saw everything as a game, and everyone as a toy.

But not everyone was amused by the jester's antics. Some people were angry, scared, or frustrated by the disruption of their lives. They tried to stop the jester, or to escape from its influence. They called the police, the army, and the scientists, but none of them could do anything against the jester's power.

Among the people who encountered the jester, there were some who reacted differently. They were not afraid or annoyed by the jester's tricks. They were amused, intrigued, or fascinated by them. They saw the jester as a challenge, an opportunity, or a friend. They decided to play along with the jester, or to learn from it.

One of them was Alice, a young girl who loved adventure and imagination. She saw the jester as a hero from her favorite stories, who came to make the world more interesting and fun. She followed the jester around the city, enjoying its pranks and jokes. She even helped the jester with some of its schemes, using her own creativity and wit.

Another one was Bob, an old man who hated his boring and lonely life. He saw the jester as a savior from his misery and despair. He welcomed the jester's changes to his reality, finding them more exciting and meaningful than his routine and dull existence. He let go of his fears and regrets and embraced the jester's surprises and challenges.

A third one was Carol, a young woman who was curious about everything and anything. She saw the jester as a teacher from another dimension, who came to show her new perspectives and possibilities. She studied the jester's powers and methods, trying to understand how they worked and why they existed. She asked the jester questions and listened to its answers.

The Cosmic Jester noticed these three people among the crowd. It was intrigued by their reactions to its presence and actions. It decided to pay more attention to them, and to test them further. It invited them to join its game, promising them rewards if they succeeded.

The game was simple: The jester would create three scenarios for each of them, each one more difficult than the last. They had to overcome each scenario using their own skills and abilities. If they failed in any scenario, they would lose the game. If they completed all three scenarios, they would win the game.

The first scenario for Alice was a maze of mirrors. The jester trapped her inside a labyrinth of reflective surfaces that distorted her vision and sense of direction. She had to find her way out before she got lost or went mad.

Alice was not afraid of the maze. She loved puzzles and riddles and saw this as an opportunity to test her intelligence and intuition. She used her logic and memory to remember where she had been and where she had not been. She used her imagination and creativity to find clues and patterns in the mirrors. She used her courage and determination to keep going despite the confusion and frustration.

She eventually found the exit of the maze, where the jester was waiting for her with applause.

"Bravo! Bravo! You did it!" The jester said with admiration.

"Thank you! Thank you! That was fun!" Alice said with excitement.

"You're welcome! You're welcome! But don't get too cocky! That was only the first challenge! The next one will be harder!" The jester said with a wink.

"I'm ready! I'm ready! Bring it on!" Alice said with confidence.

The first scenario for Bob was a haunted house. The jester transported him to an old mansion that was filled with ghosts and monsters that tried to scare him or harm him. He had to survive until dawn without losing his sanity or his life.

Bob was not scared of the house. He had nothing to lose in his life, and nothing to fear in death. He saw this as an opportunity to test his strength and endurance. He used his experience and wisdom to avoid or fight the creatures that attacked him. He used his humor and sarcasm to mock and taunt the ones that tried to frighten him. He used his will and faith to keep calm and hopeful despite the horror and danger.

He eventually made it to the morning, where the jester was waiting for him with a smile.

"Well done! Well done! You did it!" The jester said with respect.

"Thank you! Thank you! That was thrilling!" Bob said with relief.

"You're welcome! You're welcome! But don't get too comfortable! That was only the first challenge! The next one will be harder!" The jester said with a grin.

"I'm ready! I'm ready! Bring it on!" Bob said with courage.

The first scenario for Carol was a paradox. The jester created a situation that defied logic and reason, where nothing made sense, and everything contradicted itself. She had to find a way to resolve the paradox without losing her mind or her reality.

Carol was not confused by the paradox. She loved mysteries and anomalies and saw this as an opportunity to test her knowledge and curiosity. She used her observation and analysis to identify and examine the elements of the paradox. She used her experimentation and hypothesis to test and modify the variables of the paradox. She used her logic and intuition to find a solution or an explanation for the paradox.

She eventually found a way to break the paradox, where the jester was waiting for her with a nod.

"Very good! Very good! You did it!" The jester said with appreciation.

"Thank you! Thank you! That was fascinating!" Carol said with satisfaction.

"You're welcome! You're welcome! But don't get too smug! That was only the first challenge! The next one will be harder!" The jester said with a smirk.

"I'm ready! I'm ready! Bring it on!" Carol said with curiosity.

The second scenario for Alice was a fairy tale. The jester transformed her into a princess who was trapped in a tower by a wicked witch. She had to escape from the tower and defeat the witch, with the help of a handsome prince.

Alice was not impressed by the fairy tale. She did not like stories that were cliché and predictable and saw this as an insult to her intelligence and imagination. She used her wit and charm to trick the witch and the prince, making them think that she was a helpless and naive damsel. She used her skills and resources to find a way out of the tower, using whatever she could find or make. She used her bravery and independence to confront and defeat the witch, without relying on anyone else.

She eventually freed herself from the tower, where the jester was waiting for her with surprise.

"Wow! Wow! You did it!" The jester said with astonishment.

"Thank you! Thank you! That was easy!" Alice said with disdain.

"You're welcome! You're welcome! But don't get too arrogant! That was only the second challenge! The next one will be harder!" The jester said with a frown.

"I'm ready! I'm ready! Bring it on!" Alice said with defiance.

The second scenario for Bob was a war zone. The jester transported him to a battlefield where he was caught in the middle of a violent conflict between two armies. He had to survive the war without getting killed or captured, while choosing a side to fight for.

Bob was not bothered by the war zone. He had seen enough violence and suffering in his life and saw this as an opportunity to test his morals and values. He used his compassion and humanity to help the innocent and wounded, regardless of their affiliation. He used his courage and honor to fight against the unjust and cruel, regardless of their power. He used his wisdom and justice to choose a side that aligned with his principles, regardless of their odds.

He eventually survived the war, where the jester was waiting for him with admiration.

"Amazing! Amazing! You did it!" The jester said with respect.

"Thank you! Thank you! That was meaningful!" Bob said with gratitude.

"You're welcome! You're welcome! But don't get too sentimental! That was only the second challenge! The next one will be harder!" The jester said with a smile.

"I'm ready! I'm ready! Bring it on!" Bob said with determination.

The second scenario for Carol was a riddle. The jester presented her with a question that seemed impossible to answer or had multiple answers that were equally valid. She had to find the correct answer, or prove that there was no correct answer, without giving up or cheating.

Carol was not stumped by the riddle. She loved challenges and puzzles and saw this as an opportunity to test her logic and creativity. She used her reasoning and deduction to eliminate the wrong or inconsistent answers, or to find flaws or loopholes in the question. She used her imagination and innovation to generate new or alternative answers, or to reframe or redefine the question. She used her confidence and persistence to keep trying until she found a satisfactory answer or proved that there was none.

She eventually solved the riddle, where the jester was waiting for her with approval.

"Excellent! Excellent! You did it!" The jester said with appreciation.

"Thank you! Thank you! That was intriguing!" Carol said with delight.

"You're welcome! You're welcome! But don't get too confident! That was only the second challenge! The next one will be harder!" The jester said with a wink.

"I'm ready! I'm ready! Bring it on!" Carol said with eagerness.

The third scenario for Alice was a nightmare. The jester created a world that was based on her deepest fears and insecurities. She had to face her own demons and overcome them, without losing her sanity or her identity.

Alice was terrified by the nightmare. She hated things that were scary and painful and saw this as a threat to her happiness and freedom. She used her optimism and hope to fight against the despair and darkness that surrounded her. She used her love and friendship to support and protect the people she cared about, who were also in danger. She used her self-esteem and courage to confront and accept the parts of herself that she feared or hated, without letting them define or destroy her.

She eventually woke up from the nightmare, where the jester was waiting for her with respect.

"Congratulations! Congratulations! You did it!" The jester said with sincerity.

"Thank you! Thank you! That was hard!" Alice said with relief.

"You're welcome! You're welcome! But don't get too relaxed! That was only the third challenge! The final one will be harder!" The jester said with a smile.

"I'm ready! I'm ready! Bring it on!" Alice said with determination.

The third scenario for Bob was a utopia. The jester created a world that was based on his ideal vision of happiness and peace. He had to enjoy his perfect life without getting bored or complacent, while keeping his integrity and identity.

Bob was delighted by the utopia. He loved things that were pleasant and satisfying and saw this as a reward for his hardships and sacrifices. He used his gratitude and joy to appreciate and celebrate the good things that he had. He used his generosity and kindness to share and spread happiness to others, who were also content. He used his humility and wisdom to remember and learn from his past, without letting it haunt or limit him.

He eventually left the utopia, where the jester was waiting for him with admiration.

"Fantastic! Fantastic! You did it!" The jester said with sincerity.

"Thank you! Thank you! That was wonderful!" Bob said with joy.

"You're welcome! You're welcome! But don't get too comfortable! That was only the third challenge! The final one will be harder!" The jester said with a smile.

"I'm ready! I'm ready! Bring it on!" Bob said with confidence.

The third scenario for Carol was a mystery. The jester created a world that was based on a complex and intriguing problem that needed to be solved. She had to find the solution without getting lost or distracted, while using all her skills and knowledge.

Carol was fascinated by the mystery. She loved things that were challenging and interesting and saw this as an opportunity to test her intelligence and curiosity. She used her observation and analysis to collect and examine the clues and evidence that were available. She used her experimentation and hypothesis to test and modify the theories and solutions that were possible. She used her logic and intuition to find the best answer, or to prove that there was none.

She eventually solved the mystery, where the jester was waiting for her with respect.

"Brilliant! Brilliant! You did it!" The jester said with sincerity.

"Thank you! Thank you! That was captivating!" Carol said with satisfaction.

"You're welcome! You're welcome! But don't get too smug! That was only the third challenge! The final one will be harder!" The jester said with a smile.

"I'm ready! I'm ready! Bring it on!" Carol said with curiosity.

The final scenario for Alice, Bob, and Carol was a choice. The jester brought them together and presented them with a dilemma. They had to choose between staying in the jester's world, where they could have anything they wanted, or returning to their own world, where they had to face their own problems. They had to make the choice individually and collectively, without knowing what the others would choose.

Alice, Bob, and Carol were conflicted by the choice. They liked the jester's world, where they had fun, excitement, and learning. They did not like their own world, where they had boredom, misery, and ignorance. But they also knew that the jester's world was not real, and that their own world was not hopeless. They had to weigh the pros and cons of each option and decide what was best for them and for each other.

They eventually made their choice, where the jester was waiting for them with curiosity

"So? So? What did you choose?" The jester asked eagerly.

"We chose..." Alice, Bob, and Carol said in unison.

"We chose to return to our world." Alice, Bob, and Carol said in unison.

"Really? Really? Why?" The jester asked with surprise.

"Because we learned a lot from you, but we also learned a lot about ourselves. We realized that we could make our own world more fun, exciting, and interesting, by using our imagination, courage, and curiosity. We also realized that we have people who care about us, and who need us, in our own world. We don't want to abandon them, or ourselves, for a fantasy. We want to live in reality and make it better." Alice, Bob, and Carol explained.

"I see. I see. I understand. I respect your choice. You are very brave and wise. I'm proud of you." The jester said with sincerity.

"Thank you. Thank you. We appreciate your game. You are very powerful and funny. We're grateful to you." Alice, Bob, and Carol said with sincerity.

"You're welcome. You're welcome. I enjoyed your company. You are very smart and creative. I'll miss you." The jester said with sincerity.

"We'll miss you too. We'll miss you too. But maybe we'll see you again someday. Maybe in another game." Alice, Bob, and Carol said with hope.

"Maybe. Maybe. Who knows? Anything is possible." The jester said with a smile.

The jester then opened a portal that led back to their own world. Alice, Bob, and Carol hugged the jester goodbye, and thanked it again for the experience. They then walked through the portal, holding hands.

The jester watched them go with a smile and a tear. It then closed the portal, and flew away to find another world to play in.

The Master of Nothing

There was once a master who claimed to know nothing. He said that he had no knowledge, no wisdom, no skill, no talent, no virtue, no merit. He said that he was the master of nothing.

Many people were curious about him and wanted to learn from him. They came to his hut and asked him questions, hoping to hear his teachings. But the master always answered them with silence, or with nonsense, or with laughter.

Some people thought that he was hiding his true knowledge, and that he was testing their patience and sincerity. They stayed with him for a long time, waiting for him to reveal his secrets. But the master never did.

Some people thought that he was mocking them, and that he was playing with their minds and emotions. They got angry and frustrated with him, and they left him in disgust. But the master did not care.

Some people thought that he was crazy, and that he had lost his sanity and reason. They pitied and feared him, and they avoided him as much as possible. But the master did not mind.

Some people thought that he was enlightened, and that he had transcended all concepts and distinctions. They revered and admired him, and they followed him as his disciples. But the master did not notice.

The master lived his life as he pleased, doing nothing and everything, knowing nothing and everything, being nothing and everything. He was the master of nothing, and nothing was his master.

The Contradiction Sage

He was known as the Contradiction Sage, a wise and mysterious man who lived in a cave on the top of a mountain. He was sought by many seekers of truth, who wanted to learn from his wisdom and experience. He was also feared by many authorities, who wanted to silence his voice and challenge his influence. He was a man of contradictions, who spoke in paradoxes and riddles, who taught in opposites and extremes, who lived in harmony and conflict.

He was a man of truth.

He had a rule for those who wanted to meet him: they had to climb the mountain and reach his cave, without any help or guidance. They had to face the dangers and difficulties of the journey, without any protection or comfort. They had to prove their sincerity and determination, without any doubt or hesitation.

He had a test for those who reached his cave: they had to ask him one question, and one question only. They had to ask him the most important question of their lives, the question that haunted them or inspired them, the question that defined them or challenged them.

He had an answer for those who asked him their question: he would answer them with another question, a question that contradicted their question, a question that exposed their assumptions or beliefs, a question that opened their minds or hearts.

He had a lesson for those who answered his question: he would teach them the meaning of contradiction, the value of paradox, the power of riddle. He would teach them that truth is not absolute or relative, but both. He would teach them that reality is not fixed or changing, but both. He would teach them that life is not good or bad, but both.

He would teach them contradiction.

He met many people, from all walks of life, who came to his cave with their questions. He met a king who asked him how to rule his kingdom, a priest who asked him how to serve his god, a scholar who asked him how to acquire knowledge, a warrior who asked him how to win battles, a lover who asked him how to find happiness.

He answered them with his questions: he asked the king why he wanted to rule, he asked the priest who his god was, he asked the scholar what he knew, he asked the warrior what he fought for, he asked the lover what he loved.

He taught them his lessons: he taught the king that ruling is not about power or control, but about service and responsibility, he taught the priest that god is not about dogma or faith, but about mystery and wonder, he taught the scholar that knowledge is not about facts or theories, but about questions and curiosity, he taught the warrior that winning is not about violence or victory, but about peace and harmony, he taught the lover that happiness is not about pleasure or satisfaction, but about love and compassion.

He taught them contradiction.

He told them his stories, and they listened. Some of them were enlightened by his stories, some of them were confused by his stories, some of them were angry at his stories. Some of them understood what he was trying to say, some of them misunderstood what he was trying to say, some of them ignored what he was trying to say. Some of them thanked him and became his friends, some of them left him and went their own ways, some of them tried to kill him or capture him.

He didn't care. He just kept telling his stories.

Join the Laughter Revolution

Max and Mia have been best friends since kindergarten. They shared everything: their toys, their secrets, their dreams. They also shared a love for comedy. They watched every sitcom, stand-up show, and sketch they could find. They made each other laugh with their jokes, impressions, and pranks. They dreamed of becoming famous comedians someday.

But their world changed when the Great Crisis hit. A global pandemic, an economic collapse, a political turmoil. Everything went wrong at once. People lost their jobs, their homes, their hope. Laughter became a rare commodity. Fear and despair took over.

Max and Mia refused to give up on their dream. They decided to start a podcast called "Join the Laughter Revolution". They wanted to spread some joy and humor in these dark times. They recorded their episodes in Max's basement, using his old laptop and microphone. They talked about anything and everything: current events, pop culture, personal stories. They made fun of the absurdity and irony of life. They invited guests who had inspiring or funny stories to share. They encouraged their listeners to laugh at themselves and the world.

They didn't have many followers at first. But slowly, their podcast gained popularity. People started to tune in every week, eager to hear their witty and hilarious commentary. People started to write to them, thanking them for making them smile and laugh. People started to call them "the heroes of comedy".

Max and Mia were thrilled. They felt like they were making a difference. They felt like they were living their dream.

But they also faced challenges. Some people didn't like their podcast. Some people thought they were disrespectful, insensitive, or subversive. Some people wanted to silence them, censor them, or punish them.

One of these people was General Stone, the leader of the New Order, a radical faction that seized power in the country after the Great Crisis. He hated comedy. He hated laughter. He hated anything that challenged his authority or his vision of the world.

He saw Max and Mia as a threat. He saw them as enemies of the state.

He decided to put an end to their podcast.

And he decided to put an end to them.

Max and Mia were recording their latest episode when they heard a loud knock on the door.

"Who is it?" Max asked, pausing the recording.

"It's the New Order. Open up!" a voice shouted from outside.

Max and Mia exchanged a look of horror. They knew what this meant. They had heard stories of people who were arrested, tortured, or killed by the New Order for speaking their minds or expressing their opinions.

They quickly grabbed their laptop and microphone and ran to the back door. They hoped to escape through the backyard and find a safe place to hide.

But they were too late. As soon as they opened the door, they saw a group of armed soldiers waiting for them. They pointed their guns at them and ordered them to surrender.

"Max and Mia, you are under arrest for crimes against the state. You have been spreading lies, propaganda, and sedition through your podcast. You have been inciting rebellion and disorder among the people. You have been mocking and insulting the glorious leader, General Stone. You have been violating the laws of the New Order. You have no right to laugh. You have no right to speak. You have no right to live."

Max and Mia were stunned. They couldn't believe this was happening. They had never hurt anyone. They had never intended to cause any trouble. They had only wanted to make people laugh.

They tried to reason with the soldiers. They tried to explain that their podcast was just a joke, a satire, a parody. They tried to appeal to their humanity, their compassion, their sense of humor.

But it was useless. The soldiers were brainwashed by the New Order. They had no empathy, no sympathy, no emotion. They only followed orders.

They dragged Max and Mia to their truck and threw them inside. They locked the doors and drove away.

Max and Mia looked at each other with fear and sadness. They didn't know where they were going. They didn't know what would happen to them. They didn't know if they would ever see each other again.

They held hands and tried to comfort each other.

"Hey, don't worry. We'll get out of this somehow. We always do." Max said, trying to sound optimistic.

"Yeah, you're right. We're not going to let them break us. We're not going to let them take away our laughter." Mia said, trying to sound brave.

They smiled weakly and squeezed each other's hands.

They remembered all the good times they had together. All the jokes they made.

All the laughs they shared. All the dreams they chased.

They remembered why they started their podcast in the first place. To bring some light and hope to a dark and hopeless world. To join the laughter revolution.

They decided to keep their spirits up. They decided to keep their humor alive.

They decided to keep their podcast going.

They whispered jokes and stories into each other's ears. They giggled and snorted quietly. They ignored the angry glares and threats from the soldiers.

They made each other laugh.

And they hoped that someone, somewhere, was listening.

The truck arrived at a large, gray building surrounded by barbed wire and guard towers. It was the headquarters of the New Order, where General Stone ruled with an iron fist.

The soldiers dragged Max and Mia out of the truck and pushed them into the building. They walked through a long corridor filled with cells and torture chambers. They saw people who were beaten, bruised, and bloodied. They heard screams, cries, and moans. They smelled fear, pain, and death.

They felt a chill run down their spines. They knew they were in hell.

They were taken to a large room where a man was sitting behind a desk. He was wearing a black uniform with medals and badges. He had a stern face, a scarred cheek, and a cold eye. He was General Stone.

He looked at Max and Mia with contempt and disgust. He recognized them from their podcast. He hated them more than anyone else.

He spoke in a harsh and authoritative voice.

"So, you are the infamous Max and Mia. The so-called heroes of comedy. The traitors of the state. The enemies of the New Order."

He paused and sneered.

"I have been waiting for this moment for a long time. I have been listening to your podcast every week, hoping to find a clue to your location. I have been tracking your signals, tracing your calls, hacking your accounts. I have been hunting you down like rats."

He leaned forward and glared at them. "And now I have you. And now you will pay for your crimes."

He pressed a button on his desk and a large screen lit up behind him. It showed images and clips from their podcast. It showed them making jokes about him, his policies, his followers. It showed them laughing at his face, his voice, his name.

He pointed at the screen and shouted. "Look at this! Look at what you have done! You have insulted me, the supreme leader of this nation! You have ridiculed me, the savior of this world! You have defied me, the master of this order!"

He slammed his fist on his desk and roared.

"You have committed the ultimate sin! You have dared to laugh at me!"

He stood up and walked towards them. He grabbed them by their collars and lifted them up. He brought them close to his face and spat.

"You think you are funny? You think you are clever? You think you are brave? You are nothing but fools. Pathetic, worthless, miserable fools."

He threw them on the floor and kicked them.

"You have no idea what you have done. You have no idea what you have unleashed. You have no idea what I will do to you."

He walked back to his desk and pressed another button. A door opened and two men entered the room. They were wearing white coats and carrying syringes.

They were the doctors of the New Order.

They were the experts of mind control.

They were the agents of laughter suppression.

General Stone pointed at Max and Mia and ordered the doctors.

"Take them away. Erase their memories. Destroy their personalities. Eliminate their humor. Make them obedient. Make them silent. Make them mine."

The doctors nodded and approached Max and Mia. They grabbed them by their arms and dragged them towards the door.

Max and Mia struggled and resisted. They tried to break free and fight back.

They tried to scream and shout.

But it was no use. The soldiers held them down and injected them with the syringes.

They felt a sharp pain in their veins. They felt a numbness in their brains. They felt a darkness in their souls.

They felt their laughter fading away.

They looked at each other with tears in their eyes. They tried to remember each other's names, faces, voices. They tried to remember their jokes, stories, and dreams.

They tried to remember why they laughed.

But they couldn't.

They forgot everything.

They became nothing.

The Absurd Mentor

Alex was a young and ambitious writer who wanted to make a name for himself in the literary world. He had talent and passion, but he lacked experience and guidance. He wanted to find a mentor, someone who could teach him the secrets of the craft, someone who could help him achieve his dreams.

He had heard of a famous and eccentric writer who lived in a secluded cabin in the woods. He had read his books, which were full of absurd and surreal stories that defied logic and reason. He admired his style, which was witty and original.

He had decided to seek him out, to ask him to be his mentor.

He had found his address, packed his bags, and drove to the cabin. He knocked on the door and waited.

The door opened and a man appeared. He was old and thin, with a long beard and a wild look in his eyes. He wore a hat made of feathers and a coat made of newspapers. He smiled and said: "Hello, stranger. What brings you to my humble abode?"

Alex was surprised by his appearance, but he tried to be polite.

"Hello, sir. My name is Alex. I'm a writer, and I'm a big fan of your work. I came here to ask you a favor."

The man raised his eyebrows.

"A favor? What kind of favor?"

Alex took a deep breath and said:

"I want you to be my mentor. I want you to teach me how to write like you, how to create absurd and surreal stories that captivate the readers."

The man laughed.

"Ha! You want me to be your mentor? You want me to teach you how to write absurd and surreal stories? That's a very bold request, my friend. Why should I do that?"

Alex felt nervous, but he tried to be confident.

"Because you are the best at what you do, sir. Because you have a unique vision and voice that no one else can match. Because you have inspired me and many others with your stories. Because I have potential and passion, and I want to learn from you."

The man nodded.

"I see. You are very flattering, my friend. But flattery will not get you far with me. You see, I don't take students lightly. I don't teach anyone who asks me. I only teach those who are worthy, those who can prove themselves, those who can pass my test."

Alex felt curious.

"Your test? What kind of test?"

The man smiled.

"A very simple test, my friend. A very simple test indeed. All you have to do is answer one question."

Alex felt relieved.

"One question? That's it? That doesn't sound too hard."

The man nodded.

"Yes, one question. But not just any question. A very special question. A very absurd question."

Alex felt intrigued.

"An absurd question? What do you mean?"

The man said:

"I mean a question that has no answer, or many answers, or contradictory answers. A question that makes no sense, or too much sense, or different senses. A question that challenges your perception of reality and your ability to think creatively."

Alex felt confused.

"Can you give me an example?"

The man said:

"Sure. Here's an example: How many angels can dance on the head of a pin?"

Alex felt puzzled.

"That's an absurd question?"

The man said:

"Yes, it is. It's an old theological question that has been debated for centuries by scholars and philosophers. It's an absurd question because it assumes that angels exist, that they can dance, that they have size and shape, that they can fit on a pinhead, that there is a limit to their number, etc. It's an absurd question because it has no definitive answer, or many possible answers, or contradictory answers."

Alex felt curious.

"So how would you answer it?"

The man said:

"I wouldn't answer it at all. I would reject it as meaningless and irrelevant. Or I would answer it with another absurd question, such as: How many pins can fit on the head of an angel? Or I would answer it with an absurd statement, such as: "Angels don't dance on pinheads, they dance on disco balls."

Alex felt amused.

"I see. That's very clever."

The man said:

"Thank you. But enough about me. Let's talk about you. Are you ready for your test?"

Alex felt nervous.

"Yes, I am."

The man said:

"Good. Then here is your question: Why is a raven like a writing desk?"

Alex recognized the question. It was from Alice in Wonderland, one of his favorite books. It was a question that the Mad Hatter asked Alice, and never gave her an answer. It was a question that had puzzled and amused many readers for generations. It was a question that had no answer, or many answers, or contradictory answers. It was an absurd question.

Alex thought for a moment. He tried to think of a way to answer the question, or to avoid the question, or to challenge the question. He tried to think of something clever, something witty, something original. He tried to think of something that would impress the man, something that would show him his potential and passion, something that would make him his mentor.

He opened his mouth and said:

"Because they both have quills."

The man frowned.

"Wrong," he said. "That is not an absurd answer. That is a logical answer. That is a boring answer. That is an answer that has been given before by many others. You have failed the test. You are not worthy to be my student. Please leave now and never come back."

Alex felt a wave of shock and disappointment. How could he be wrong? He had given an answer that made sense, that was clever, that was original. He had given an answer that he thought was good, or at least good enough.

He tried to protest, but the man cut him off.

"Silence," he said. "There is no room for argument or explanation here. You have failed, and that is final. Now go, before I have to force you out."

Alex felt tears in his eyes as he got up from his chair. He looked at the man and hoped to find some sympathy or support, but he only saw contempt and disappointment. He felt alone and humiliated as he walked out of the cabin, leaving behind his dreams of becoming a writer.

He wondered what he had done wrong, what he had missed, what he had misunderstood. He wondered if there was any point in pursuing writing anymore, if it was all a lie or a joke or a trap. He wondered if there was any meaning or order in this absurd world, or if it was all just random and cruel.

He wondered if he would ever find peace.

The Discordian Circus

The day the circus came to town, everything changed.

It was a sunny morning in May, and the town of Harmony was living up to its name. The streets were clean and quiet, the shops were open and busy, the people were friendly and polite. Harmony was a place where everyone knew each other, where everyone followed the rules, where everyone was happy.

Or so they thought.

The circus arrives without warning, without invitation, without permission. It was a caravan of colorful wagons, pulled by strange animals and driven by even stranger people. They wore masks and costumes, they played instruments and sang songs, they laughed and joked and danced. They looked like they had come from another world.

And maybe they had.

They set up their tents on the outskirts of town, near the old, abandoned factory. They hung banners and posters, announcing their name and their show.

The Discordian Circus.

The Greatest Show on Earth.

The Show that Will Change Your Life.

They invited everyone to come and see them. They promised wonders and miracles, thrills and chills, fun and games.

They promised chaos and absurdity.

Some of the townspeople were curious. Some of them were bored. Some of them were adventurous. Some of them were rebellious.

They decided to go and see the circus.

They didn't know what they were getting into.

They didn't know what they would find.

They didn't know who they would become.

"Wow, look at this place!" said Alice, a young waitress who had always dreamed of traveling the world. She dragged her boyfriend Tom, a mechanic who liked to fix things, to the entrance of the circus. "It's so colorful and lively! I can't wait to see what's inside!"

"I don't know, Alice," said Tom, looking around nervously. "This doesn't look like any circus I've ever seen. It looks weird and creepy. Maybe we should go back."

"Oh, come on, Tom. Don't be such a chicken. Where's your sense of adventure? Where's your sense of fun? This is a once in a lifetime opportunity! Let's go and have some fun!"

She bought two tickets from a man wearing a monkey mask and a fez. He smiled at them with his yellow teeth and handed them two balloons.

"Welcome to the Discordian Circus!" he said in a high-pitched voice. "The greatest show on earth! The show that will change your life! Enjoy your stay!"

He winked at them and pointed to a sign that read:

ENTER AT YOUR OWN RISK

Alice laughed and pulled Tom inside the tent. Tom gulped and followed her reluctantly.

They entered a world of wonders and horrors.

A world of sights and sounds, of colors and shapes, of illusions and realities.

A world of freaks and geeks, of clowns and acrobats, of magicians and fortune tellers.

A world of comedy and tragedy, of romance and horror, of satire and parody.

A world that made them laugh and cry, that made them gasp and scream, which made them think and feel.

A world that made them question everything.

"Look at that!" Alice exclaimed as she saw a man with three heads juggling knives. "That's amazing!"

"That's impossible!" Tom said as he saw a woman with six arms playing the piano. "That's unnatural!"

"Look at this!" Alice said as she saw a clown with a rubber nose making balloon animals. "That's hilarious!"

"That's stupid!" Tom said as he saw a mime with a painted face pretending to be trapped in a box. "That's boring!"

"Look at us!" Alice said as she saw their reflections in a distorted mirror. "We look so funny!"

"We look so ugly!" Tom said as he saw their faces twisted and stretched. "We look so ridiculous!"

They argued and bickered as they walked through the circus. They disagreed on everything they saw. They had different opinions, different tastes, different reactions.

They realized they had nothing in common.

They realized they didn't love each other anymore.

They broke up in front of a fortune teller who told them their future was doomed.

They left the circus separately, feeling angry and sad.

They never saw each other again.

The circus changed them. It changed their minds, their hearts, their souls. It changed their relationship, their career, their life. It changed their town.

It changed their world.

Some of them loved it. Some of them hated it. Some of them feared it. Some of them embraced it.

But none of them could ignore it.

None of them could forget it.

None of them could escape it.

The circus stayed in town for a week. Then it packed up its tents and left as mysteriously as it had arrived.

But it left behind a legacy.

A legacy of discord.

A legacy of laughter.

The Quest for the Erisian Relic

The quest began with a letter.

A letter that arrived in a pineapple.

A letter that was written in crayon.

A letter that said:

Dear Adventurers,

You have been chosen to participate in the most important and exciting quest of your lives. You have been selected to find the Erisian Relic, the most powerful and mysterious artifact in the world. The Erisian Relic is a golden apple with the word "Kallisti" inscribed on it, which means "to the prettiest one". It was created by Eris, the goddess of chaos and discord, and it has the ability to cause mayhem and madness wherever it goes. It has been hidden for centuries in a secret location, guarded by traps and puzzles and riddles. Only the bravest and cleverest adventurers can hope to reach it and claim its power.

Are you brave enough? Are you clever enough? Are you ready for the adventure of a lifetime?

If you are, then follow these instructions:

1. Meet me at the Pineapple Inn at noon tomorrow. Look for a man wearing a pink tutu and a sombrero. He will give you further details.

2. Bring with you a backpack, a flashlight, a compass, a banana, and a rubber duck. You will need them for the quest.

3. Do not tell anyone about this letter or this quest. It is a secret and dangerous mission. Trust no one.

4. Do not be afraid of anything. Fear is the mind-killer. Embrace the absurd.

5. Have fun.

Sincerely

The Jester

P.S. This is not a joke.

The letter was signed with a smiley face.

The letter was addressed to four people:
- Jack, a rogue who liked to steal things and flirt with women.
- Jill, a mage who liked to cast spells and read books.
- Bob, a warrior who liked to fight monsters and drink beer.
- Sue, a cleric who liked to heal wounds and pray to gods.

They were all friends and adventurers who had met in various quests and missions. They had shared many dangers and joys together. They had also received many letters from mysterious sources before, inviting them to join various quests and missions. They were used to such things.

But this letter was different.

This letter intrigued them.

This letter challenged them.

This letter tempted them.

They decided to accept it.

They decided to go on the quest.

They decided to find the Erisian Relic.

They packed their bags, grabbed their weapons, and headed to the Pineapple Inn.

They didn't know what they were getting into.

They didn't know what they would find.

They didn't know who they would become.

They met the man in the pink tutu and the sombrero at the Pineapple Inn. He was sitting at a table, eating a slice of pineapple pizza. He smiled at them and waved his hand.

"Hello, hello, hello!" he said cheerfully. "You must be Jack, Jill, Bob, and Sue! I'm so glad you came! I'm the Jester, your guide for this quest!"

He stood up and bowed gracefully.

"Welcome to the quest for the Erisian Relic! The greatest quest of all time! The quest that will change your lives! Are you ready to begin?"

He didn't wait for their answer. He grabbed their hands and dragged them outside.

"Come on, come on, come on! Let's go, let's go, let's go! Adventure awaits!"

He led them to a wagon parked outside the inn. It was painted with bright colors and covered with stickers and graffiti. It had a sign that read:

THE JESTER'S WAGON

THE FASTEST AND FUNNIEST WAY TO TRAVEL

HOP IN AND HOLD ON

The Jester opened the door and pushed them inside.

"Get in, get in, get in! This is our ride for this quest! It's fast, it's fun, it's fabulous!

It can take us anywhere we want to go!"

He jumped in after them and closed the door.

"Are you ready?" he asked excitedly.

"Ready for what?" Jack asked suspiciously.

"Ready for this!" The Jester said as he pressed a button on the dashboard.

The wagon started to shake and rumble. The windows turned black. The lights flashed on and off. The speakers blasted loud music.

The wagon took off like a rocket.

The adventurers screamed as they felt themselves being lifted off the ground and hurled into space.

They looked out the windows and saw stars and planets zooming past them.

They looked at each other and saw fear and confusion on their faces.

They looked at the Jester and saw joy and madness on his face.

He laughed maniacally as he steered the wagon through the cosmos.

"Welcome to the quest for the Erisian Relic!" he shouted. "The quest that will take you to the most amazing and bizarre places in the universe! The quest that will test your courage and intelligence and creativity! The quest that will make you laugh and cry and scream and wonder! The quest that will make you question everything you know and believe! The quest that will make you embrace the absurd!"

He pointed to a sign above the door that read:

THE QUEST FOR THE ERISIAN RELIC

RULES:

1. THERE ARE NO RULES

2. EXPECT THE UNEXPECTED

3. HAVE FUN

He winked at them and said "Are you ready for the adventure of a lifetime?"

They weren't.

But they had no choice.

They were on the quest.

They were on the quest for the Erisian Relic.

The wagon flew through space for a while, until it reached a large wormhole. The Jester pointed at it and said "Here we go! Our first destination! The Realm of the Riddle Master!"

He drove the wagon into the wormhole and disappeared.

The adventurers felt a surge of energy and a twist of reality. They closed their eyes and held their breath.

They opened their eyes and gasped.

They were in a different world.

A world of puzzles and games, of questions and answers, of logic and paradox.

A world where everything was a riddle.

They saw a landscape of giant chess boards and crossword grids, of mazes and labyrinths, of sudoku and Rubik's cubes. They saw buildings made of cards and dominoes, of dice and coins, of letters and numbers. They saw people wearing hats and masks, carrying books and pens, speaking in rhymes and codes.

They saw the Riddle Master.

He was sitting on a throne made of puzzle pieces, wearing a crown made of question marks. He had a long beard and a long pipe, a monocle and a cane. He looked like a cross between a wizard and a professor.

He smiled at them and said: "Welcome to my realm, dear adventurers. I'm the Riddle Master, the lord of this land. I'm glad you came to visit me. I've been expecting you."

He gestured to the wagon and said: "I see you've met my friend, the Jester. He's quite a character, isn't he? He's the one who brought you here. He's the one who told me about you. He's the one who challenged me to test you."

He leaned forward and said: "You see, Jester and I have a little bet going on. He bets that you can solve my riddles and find the Erisian Relic. I bet that you can't. And the stakes are high. If you win, you get to keep the Relic and its power. If you lose, you lose your minds and your souls."

He laughed wickedly and said: "So, are you ready to play my game? Are you ready to face my riddles? Are you ready to risk it all?"

He didn't wait for their answer. He snapped his fingers and said: "Let the game begin!"

The Riddle Master clapped his hands and said: "Here's the first riddle for you. Listen carefully and think hard. You have one minute to answer. If you answer correctly, you move on to the next riddle. If you answer incorrectly, you lose a point. If you lose all your points, you lose the game. And if you lose the game, you lose everything. Are you ready?"

He cleared his throat and said: "What is the beginning of eternity, the end of time and space, the beginning of every end, and the end of every race?"

He looked at them expectantly and said: "Tick tock, tick tock. Time is running out. What is your answer?"

The adventurers looked at each other nervously. They tried to figure out the riddle.

Jack thought it was a trick question. He said: "There is no such thing. It's impossible."

Jill thought it was a philosophical question. She said: "It's a paradox. It's beyond comprehension."

Bob thought it was a simple question. He said: "It's a word. It's easy."

Sue thought it was a clever question. She said: "It's a letter. It's obvious."

They argued and debated as the clock ticked away.

They couldn't agree on an answer.

They couldn't solve the riddle.

They ran out of time.

The Riddle Master smiled and said: "Time's up! The correct answer is...the letter E!"

He pointed to the riddle and said: "Look at it! It's right there! The letter E is the beginning of eternity, the end of time and space, the beginning of every end, and the end of every race! It's so simple and so elegant! How could you not see it?"

He shook his head and said: "I'm sorry, but you failed the first riddle. You lose one point. You have four points left. Are you ready for the next riddle?"

He didn't wait for their answer.

He said: "Here it is. Listen carefully and think hard. You have one minute to answer. If you answer correctly, you move on to the next riddle. If you answer incorrectly, you lose a point. If you lose all your points, you lose the game. And if you lose the game, you lose everything. Are you ready?"

He cleared his throat and said: "What can travel around the world while staying in one corner?"

He looked at them expectantly and said: "Tick tock, tick tock. Time is running out.

What is your answer?"

The adventurers looked at each other nervously. They tried to figure out the riddle.

Jack thought it was a nonsense question. He said: "Nothing can do that. It's illogical."

Jill thought it was a scientific question. She said: "Maybe it's something to do with gravity or magnetism or light. I don't know."

Bob thought it was a hard question. He said: "I have no clue. It's too difficult."

Sue thought it was a smart question. She said: "It's something simple and common. It's obvious."

They argued and debated as the clock ticked away.

They couldn't agree on an answer.

They couldn't solve the riddle.

They ran out of time.

The Riddle Master smiled and said: "Time's up! The correct answer is...a stamp!"

He pointed to the riddle and said: "Look at it! It's right there! A stamp can travel around the world while staying in one corner of an envelope! It's so simple and so elegant! How could you not see it?"

He shook his head and said: "I'm sorry, but you failed the second riddle. You lose one point. You have three points left. Are you ready for the next riddle?"

He didn't wait for their answer.

He said: "Here it is. Listen carefully and think hard. You have one minute to answer. If you answer correctly, you move on to the next riddle. If you answer incorrectly, you lose a point. If you lose all your points, you lose the game. And if you lose the game, you lose everything. Are you ready?"

He cleared his throat and said: "What belongs to you but everyone else uses?"

He looked at them expectantly and said: "Tick tock, tick tock. Time is running out. What is your answer?"

The adventurers looked at each other nervously. They tried to figure out the riddle.

Jack thought it was a personal question. He said: "Maybe it's something like your name or your birthday or your phone number. I don't know."

Jill thought it was a social question. She said: "Maybe it's something like your reputation or your opinion or your advice. I don't know."

Bob thought it was a practical question. He said: "Maybe it's something like your car or your house or your money. I don't know."

Sue thought it was a clever question. She said: "It's something simple and obvious. It's obvious."

They argued and debated as the clock ticked away.

They couldn't agree on an answer.

They couldn't solve the riddle.

They ran out of time.

The Riddle Master smiled and said: "Time's up! The correct answer is...your name!"

He pointed to the riddle and said: "Look at it! It's right there! Your name belongs to you but everyone else uses it! It's so simple and so elegant! How could you not see it?"

He shook his head and said: "I'm sorry, but you failed the third riddle. You lose one point. You have two points left. Are you ready for the next riddle?"

He didn't wait for their answer.

He said: "Here it is. Listen carefully and think hard. You have one minute to answer. If you answer correctly, you move on to the next riddle. If you answer incorrectly, you lose a point. If you lose all your points, you lose the game. And if you lose the game, you lose everything. Are you ready?"

He cleared his throat and said: "What is so fragile that saying its name breaks it?"

He looked at them expectantly and said: "Tick tock, tick tock. Time is running out. What is your answer?"

The adventurers looked at each other nervously. They tried to figure out the riddle.

Jack thought it was a trick question. He said: "That's impossible. Nothing can be broken by saying its name."

Jill thought it was a metaphysical question. She said: "Maybe it's something like the sound of silence or the concept of nothingness. I don't know."

Bob thought it was a hard question. He said: "I have no clue. It's too difficult."

Sue thought it was a smart question. She said: "It's something simple and obvious. It's obvious."

They argued and debated as the clock ticked away.

They couldn't agree on an answer.

They couldn't solve the riddle.

They ran out of time.

The Riddle Master smiled and said: "Time's up! The correct answer is...silence!"

He pointed to the riddle and said: "Look at it! It's right there! Silence is so fragile that saying its name breaks it! It's so simple and so elegant! How could you not see it?"

He shook his head and said: "I'm sorry, but you failed the fourth riddle. You lose one point. You have one point left. Are you ready for the final riddle?"

He didn't wait for their answer.

He said: "Here it is. Listen carefully and think hard. You have one minute to answer. If you answer correctly, you win the game. If you answer incorrectly, you lose the game. And if you lose the game, you lose everything. Are you ready?"

He cleared his throat and said: "What is the Erisian Relic?"

He looked at them expectantly and said: "Tick tock, tick tock. Time is running out. What is your answer?"

The adventurers looked at each other nervously. They tried to figure out the riddle.

Jack thought it was a joke question. He said: "That's not a riddle. That's the answer. The Erisian Relic is the Erisian Relic."

Jill thought it was a serious question. She said: "Maybe it's a symbol of chaos and discord, a source of power and danger, a mystery and a mystery. I don't know."

Bob thought it was a stupid question. He said: "I don't care. It's just a stupid apple with a stupid word on it. It's worthless."

Sue thought it was a clever question. She said: "It's something simple and obvious. It's obvious."

They argued and debated as the clock ticked away.

They couldn't agree on an answer.

They couldn't solve the riddle.

They ran out of time.

The Riddle Master smiled and said: "Time's up! The correct answer is...there is no correct answer!"

He pointed to the riddle and said: "Look at it! It's right there! The Erisian Relic is whatever you want it to be! It's whatever you think it is! It's whatever you make it to be! It's so simple and so elegant! How could you not see it?"

He shook his head and said: "I'm sorry, but you failed the final riddle. You lost the game. And you lose everything."

He snapped his fingers and said: "Goodbye, dear adventurers. It was nice meeting you."

He laughed wickedly as he watched them disappear.

They vanished into thin air.

They ceased to exist.
They lost their minds and their souls.
They lost their quest.
They lost their quest for the Erisian Relic.

The Discordian Rebellion

The year was 2077. The world was ruled by the Order, a global organization that enforced a strict set of laws and regulations on every aspect of human life. The Order claimed to have created a perfect society, where everyone was safe, secure, and productive. However, not everyone agreed with the Order's vision.

Some people felt suffocated by the lack of freedom and creativity. They longed for something more, something different, something chaotic.

These people were the discordians. They were followers of Eris, the goddess of chaos and discord. They believed that chaos was the natural state of the universe, and that order was an illusion and a tyranny. They rejected the Order's rules and sought to create their own reality, based on their whims and desires. They used pranks, hacks, art, and magic to disrupt the Order's system and spread chaos wherever they went.

The discordians were a minority, but they were growing in number and influence. They formed underground networks and communities, where they shared their ideas and resources. They communicated through secret codes and symbols, such as the golden apple and the sacred chao. They had their own rituals and ceremonies, such as the celebration of the 23rd day of each month and the invocation of the Law of Fives. They had their own scriptures and writings, such as the Principia Discordia and the Book of Eris. They had their own heroes and legends, such as Malaclypse the Younger and Omar Khayyam Ravenhurst.

The Order was aware of the discordians' existence and activities, but they underestimated their threat. They considered them to be harmless eccentrics, or at worst, minor nuisances. They thought they could control them with propaganda, surveillance, and intimidation. They were wrong.

The discordians had a plan. A plan to spark a revolution. A plan to overthrow the Order and usher in a new era of chaos. A plan that involved a secret weapon: a device that could generate a massive amount of entropy in any system it was attached to. A device that could cause anything from minor glitches to catastrophic failures. A device that could bring down the Order's infrastructure and expose its weaknesses. A device that they called the Eris Bomb.

The discordians had spent years developing and testing the Eris Bomb, using stolen or scavenged materials and components. They had hidden it in a safe location, waiting for the right moment to use it. That moment came on March 23rd, 2077: The Day of Discord.

On that day, a group of discordians infiltrated the Order's headquarters in New York City, disguised as workers or visitors. They carried with them several Eris Bombs, disguised as ordinary objects or devices. They planted them in strategic locations throughout the building, such as the power grid, the communication network, the security system, and the main computer server. Then they activated them remotely and escaped.

The effect was immediate and devastating. The Eris Bombs unleashed a wave of chaos that swept through the Order's headquarters, causing everything to malfunction or explode. The lights went out, the alarms went off, the doors locked or unlocked randomly, the elevators stopped or crashed, the fire sprinklers sprayed or burst, the phones rang or screeched, the screens flickered or flashed, the speakers blared or whispered, the computers crashed or glitched.

The Order's leaders and agents were caught off guard and panicked. They tried to restore order and control, but they failed miserably. They ran around in confusion and fear, bumping into each other or tripping over wires or debris.

Some of them tried to escape, but they found themselves trapped or lost in the darkened corridors or stairwells. Some of them tried to fight back, but they found themselves outmatched or outsmarted by the discordians' tricks or traps.

The discordians watched from a safe distance as their plan unfolded. They laughed and cheered as they saw the Order's headquarters go up in flames and smoke. They felt a surge of joy and satisfaction as they witnessed their victory over their oppressors.

They knew this was only the beginning. They knew there were more Eris Bombs hidden in other locations around the world, ready to be detonated at any time. They knew there were more discordians ready to join them in their rebellion against the Order.

They knew this was their moment.

They knew this was their time.

They knew this was their world.

Hail Eris!

All Hail Discordia!

The Discordian Detective

The city of Logos was a place where logic and reason ruled supreme. It was a place where everything was organized, structured, and predictable. It was a place where everyone followed the rules, obeyed the laws, and respected the authorities. It was a place where crime was rare, justice was swift, and order was maintained.

Or so they thought.

The city of Logos had a problem.

A problem that defied logic and reason.

A problem that disrupted organization, structure, and predictability.

A problem that broke the rules, violated the laws, and mocked the authorities.

A problem that caused crime, escaped justice, and threatened order.

The problem was a person.

A person who called himself the Discordian Detective.

The Discordian Detective was a brilliant detective with a penchant for chaos and disruption. He was a detective who solved crimes using absurd methods, confusing the traditional authorities and challenging the notion of what it meant to find order in a chaotic world.

He was a detective who left behind clues and messages that were cryptic, nonsensical, and humorous. He was a detective who used props and gadgets that were bizarre, ridiculous, and ingenious. He was a detective who wore costumes and masks that were colorful, eccentric, and expressive.

He was a detective who had fun.

And he was a detective who was very good at his job.

He solved cases that no one else could solve. He caught criminals that no one else could catch. He exposed secrets that no one else could expose.

He did it all with style and flair.

He did it all with chaos and absurdity.

He did it all with laughter and joy.

He was the Discordian Detective.

And he was the city's greatest hero.

And he was the city's greatest villain.

It depended on who you asked.

Some people loved him. Some people hated him. Some people feared him.

Some people admired him.

But no one could ignore him.

No one could forget him.

No one could stop him.

Except maybe one person.

One person who was his equal in intelligence and skill. One person who was his opposite in personality and style. One person who was his rival in profession and reputation. One person who was his friend in respect and admiration.

One person who called himself the Logical Detective.

The Logical Detective was a brilliant detective with a penchant for order and stability. He was a detective who solved crimes using rational methods, impressing the traditional authorities and reinforcing the notion of what it meant to find order in a chaotic world.

He was a detective who left behind clues and messages that were clear, sensible, and informative. He was a detective who used props and gadgets that were practical, efficient, and reliable. He was a detective who wore suits and hats that were plain, simple, and professional.

He was a detective who had no fun.

But he was a detective who was very good at his job.

He solved cases that no one else could solve. He caught criminals that no one else could catch. He exposed secrets that no one else could expose.

He did it all with precision and accuracy.

He did it all with order and stability.

He did it all with seriousness and dignity.

He was the Logical Detective.

And he was the city's greatest hero.

And he was the city's greatest villain.

It depended on who you asked.

Some people loved him. Some people hated him. Some people feared him.

Some people admired him.

But no one could ignore him.

No one could forget him.

No one could stop him.

Except maybe one person.

One person who was his equal in intelligence and skill. One person who was his opposite in personality and style. One person who was his rival in profession and reputation. One person who was his friend in respect and admiration.

One person who called himself the Discordian Detective.

The Discordian Detective and the Logical Detective had a history.

A history that began with a challenge.

A challenge that was issued by the Discordian Detective.

A challenge that was accepted by the Logical Detective.

A challenge that was simple and complex.

A challenge that was fun and serious.

A challenge that was absurd and rational.

A challenge that was this:

Whoever solved more cases in a year would be declared the best detective in the city. Whoever lost would have to admit defeat and retire from the profession.

The challenge was on.

And the city was their playground.

And their battlefield.

They competed against each other in every case. They raced against each other to find clues, suspects, and evidence. They clashed against each other in methods, strategies, and tactics. They taunted each other with messages, jokes, and insults.

They made each other better.

And they made each other worse.

They pushed each other to the limit.

And they pushed each other over the edge.

They were enemies.

And they were allies.

They were rivals.

And they were friends.

They were the Discordian Detective and the Logical Detective.

And they were the city's greatest detectives.

And they were the city's greatest problems.

The city didn't know what to do with them. The city didn't know how to handle them. The city didn't know whether to praise them or condemn them. The city didn't know whether to love them or hate them.

The city was confused.

The city was amused.

The city was entertained.

The city was annoyed.

The city was divided.

The city was united.

The city was changed.

By the Discordian Detective and the Logical Detective.

By their challenge.

By their quest.

By their game.

The game lasted for a year. A year of excitement and drama. A year of mystery and adventure. A year of chaos and order. A year of laughter and tears. A year of triumphs and failures. A year of wins and losses. A year of fun and pain. A year of life and death.

A year of stories.

Stories that were told and retold. Stories that were remembered and forgotten.

Stories that were true and false. Stories that were real and imaginary. Stories that were funny and sad. Stories that were amazing and terrible. Stories that were absurd and logical. Stories that were theirs and ours.

Stories that were the Discordian Detective's and the Logical Detective's stories.

Stories that were our stories.

Stories that ended with a twist.

A twist that was unexpected and inevitable. A twist that was shocking and satisfying. A twist that was tragic and comic. A twist that was absurd and logical.

A twist that was theirs and ours. A twist that was this:

They tied.

They solved the same number of cases in a year. They had the same score in their challenge. They had no winner or loser in their game. They had no best or worst in their profession. They had no hero or villain in their city. They had no friends or enemies in their relationship. They had no difference or similarity in their personalities. They had no chaos or order in their lives.

They had only each other.

And they had only themselves.

And they had only one choice.

To admit defeat and retire from the profession together?

Or to admit victory and continue the profession together?

To end their game?

Or to start a new game?

To stop being enemies?

Or to stop being friends?
To stop being rivals?
Or to stop being allies?
To stop being the Discordian Detective and the Logical Detective?
Or to stop being anything else?
They looked at each other and smiled.
They knew what they wanted to do.
They knew what they had to do.
They knew what they would do.
They shook hands and said "Let's do it again."

The Mirror of Discord

Leo was a normal teenager. He liked to play video games, watch movies, and hang out with his friends. He lived in a normal house, went to a normal school, and had a normal family. He was happy with his life.

Or so he thought.

Leo had a secret.

A secret that he didn't even know himself.

A secret that was hidden in his attic.

A secret that was waiting for him to discover it.

A secret that was the Mirror of Discord.

The Mirror of Discord was a mystical mirror that reflected an alternate reality filled with absurdity and randomness. It was a mirror that showed a world where nothing made sense, where anything could happen, where everything was different. It was a mirror that invited Leo to enter and explore.

And one day, he did.

It happened on a rainy afternoon, when Leo was bored and restless. He decided to go to the attic and look for something interesting. He rummaged through the boxes and bags, hoping to find an old toy or a comic book. He found nothing but junk.

He was about to give up and go back downstairs, when he saw something shiny in the corner. He walked over and saw a large mirror covered with a dusty cloth. He wondered what it was and why it was there. He pulled the cloth and revealed the mirror.

He gasped.

He saw himself in the mirror, but not as he was. He saw himself wearing a clown suit, holding a rubber chicken, and smiling widely. He blinked and rubbed his eyes, thinking he was hallucinating. He looked again and saw the same thing.

He was confused and curious.

He touched the mirror and felt a shock. He pulled his hand back and saw a spark. He heard a voice in his head.

"Hello, Leo. I'm the Mirror of Discord. I'm here to show you another world. A world of chaos and fun. A world of wonder and adventure. A world of laughter and joy. Do you want to see it?"

Leo hesitated. He didn't know what to think or what to do. He didn't know if he should trust the mirror or run away from it. He didn't know if he should be afraid or excited.

He decided to be brave.

He decided to say yes.

He decided to enter the mirror.

He stepped through the mirror and disappeared.

He entered a world of wonders and horrors.

A world of absurdity and randomness.

A world of discord.

He saw a landscape of giant mushrooms and candy canes, of rainbows and volcanoes, of clocks and balloons. He saw buildings made of cheese and chocolate, of books and bones, of cards and dominoes. He saw people wearing hats and masks, carrying umbrellas and swords, speaking in rhymes and riddles.

He saw his doppelgängers.

He saw versions of himself that were different from him in every way. He saw versions of himself that were older or younger, taller or shorter, fatter or thinner.

He saw versions of himself that had different hair colors, eye colors, skin colors.

He saw versions of himself that had different personalities, hobbies, careers.

He saw versions of himself that were absurd.

He met Leo the Clown, who made him laugh with his jokes and pranks. He met Leo the Pirate, who took him on a treasure hunt on his ship. He met Leo the Astronaut, who showed him the stars and planets on his rocket. He met Leo the Wizard, who taught him magic spells and potions on his tower.

He met many more Leos, each one more eccentric than the last.

He had fun with them.

And he learned from them.

He learned to embrace chaos and find beauty in the unpredictable.

He learned to be more creative and adventurous.

He learned to be more open-minded and tolerant.

He learned to be happier and freer.

He learned to be more himself.

He stayed in the world of discord for a while, until he felt ready to go back home. He said goodbye to his doppelgängers and thanked them for their friendship and wisdom. He walked back to the mirror and stepped through it.

He returned to his normal world.

But he was not the same Leo as before.

He was the new Leo.

A better Leo.

A happier Leo.

He looked at the mirror and smiled.

He heard the voice in his head again.

"Goodbye, Leo. I hope you enjoyed your visit. I hope you learned something valuable. I hope you had fun."

"I did," Leo said aloud. "Thank you for showing me another world. Thank you for showing me another me."

"You're welcome," the voice said. "You're always welcome here."

The voice faded away.

The mirror turned dark.

Leo left the attic and went downstairs.

He resumed his normal life.

But he never forgot his secret life.

His secret life in the Mirror of Discord.

The Chaotic Academy

Mr. Jones was not like any other teacher at the Academy. He wore colorful clothes, had a messy beard and a wide smile. He didn't follow the strict schedule, the rigid curriculum or the precise grading system. He taught whatever he felt like, whenever he felt like, however he felt like.

The students were shocked and confused. They had been trained to follow orders, memorize facts and obey rules. They had never experienced anything like Mr. Jones before. He asked them to do strange things, like draw with their eyes closed, write poems without rhyming, or act out scenes from their dreams. He encouraged them to express their opinions, feelings and ideas, even if they contradicted the official doctrine. He challenged them to think for themselves, question everything and explore the unknown.

At first, the students resisted. They complained to the principal, the parents and each other. They wanted Mr. Jones to be fired, or at least to conform to the Academy's standards. They didn't understand why he was doing this to them, or what he expected from them. They felt lost, frustrated and angry.

But gradually, something changed. Some of the students began to enjoy Mr. Jones' classes. They found them fun, exciting and liberating. They discovered new aspects of themselves, their classmates and the world. They realized that there was more to life than order and structure, that there was beauty and meaning in chaos and diversity. They started to appreciate Mr. Jones' unconventional methods, his genuine enthusiasm and his sincere care.

Soon, more and more students joined the rebellion. They began to experiment with their own styles, hobbies and interests. They formed friendships across different groups and cliques. They challenged the authority of the other teachers, the principal and the system. They demanded more freedom, creativity and individuality.

The Academy was in turmoil. The staff was divided between those who supported Mr. Jones and those who opposed him. The parents were worried about their children's future and reputation. The media was intrigued by the scandal and controversy.

But Mr. Jones was not afraid. He knew he was doing the right thing. He knew he was making a difference. He knew he was not alone.

He smiled as he entered his classroom, greeted by a chorus of cheers and applause from his students.

He said "Good morning, class! Today we are going to learn about..."

He paused for a moment, then grinned.

"...whatever you want!"

The students looked at each other, then at Mr. Jones, with a mix of surprise, curiosity and excitement. They had never been given such an opportunity before.

They had never been asked what they wanted to learn.

Some of them raised their hands, eager to share their suggestions. Others whispered among themselves, unsure of what to say. A few remained silent, still skeptical of Mr. Jones' intentions.

Mr. Jones nodded and smiled, listening to the various proposals. He heard requests for topics ranging from art and music to science and history, to sports and games. He heard questions about life and death, love and hate, war and peace. He heard expressions of wonder and doubt, hope and fear, joy and sorrow.

He was impressed by the diversity and depth of his students' interests and inquiries. He was proud of their courage and curiosity. He was happy to see them engaged and alive.

He said: "Wow, these are all great ideas! I wish we had more time to explore them all. But since we only have one hour left, let's do this: let's vote for the one topic that most of you want to learn about today. And then, let's find a way to learn about it together, using whatever resources we have available. How does that sound?"

The students agreed, some more enthusiastically than others. They quickly wrote down their preferred topic on a piece of paper, then folded it and handed it to Mr. Jones. He collected the papers, shuffled them and counted them.

He said: "And the winner is..."

He paused for dramatic effect, then announced: "...magic!"

The students gasped, some in delight, some in disbelief. Magic was a taboo topic at the Academy, a forbidden subject that was considered dangerous, irrational and heretical. It was never taught, never mentioned, never acknowledged.

But Mr. Jones was not surprised. He had expected this outcome. He had planted the seed of magic in his students' minds, subtly and gradually, through his stories, games and experiments. He had sensed their fascination and curiosity, their longing and desire, their potential and power.

He said: "Magic, huh? Well, that's a very interesting choice. And a very brave one, too. Do you know what magic is? Do you know where it comes from? Do you know how to use it?"

The students shook their heads, some eagerly, some nervously. They had no idea what magic was, or how it worked. They had only heard rumors and legends, myths and fairy tales. They had only seen glimpses and hints, sparks and flashes.

Mr. Jones said: "Well, then, let me tell you a secret: magic is real. Magic is everywhere. Magic is inside you."

He pointed at his chest, then at his students.

He said: "You have magic in your heart. You have magic in your soul. You have magic in your blood."

He raised his hand, then snapped his fingers.

He said: "And you can make magic happen."

He smiled as he watched his students' eyes widen, their mouths open, their faces glow.

He said: "But don't take my word for it. See for yourself."

He waved his hand, then pointed at the window.

He said: "Look outside."

The students turned their heads, then gasped again.

Outside the window, they saw a rainbow of colors, a symphony of sounds, a spectacle of wonders.

They saw birds and butterflies, flowers and trees, stars and clouds.

They saw dragons and unicorns, fairies and elves, mermaids and wizards.

They saw fire and water, earth and air, light and darkness.

They saw magic.

They saw themselves.

The Discordian Revolution

They called themselves the Discordians. They were the enemies of the State, the agents of chaos, the harbingers of anarchy. They wore masks of different colors and shapes, hiding their identities and expressing their individuality. They communicated through codes and symbols, using humor and irony as their weapons. They followed no leader, no doctrine, no rules. They followed only their own whims, their own visions, their own wills.

They lived in the shadows, in the cracks, in the margins. They infiltrated the system, sabotaging its functions, exposing its flaws, mocking its pretensions. They hacked into the media, broadcasting their messages, spreading their memes, creating their myths. They staged protests, riots, pranks, and art. They disrupted the order, challenged the authority, provoked the reaction.

They fought for freedom, for diversity, for creativity. They fought against oppression, conformity, and monotony. They fought for themselves, for each other, for everyone. They fought for fun, for love, for chaos.

They were hated and feared by the State, the agents of order, the defenders of stability. The State was a rigid hierarchy, a strict bureaucracy, and a totalitarian dictatorship. It controlled everything and everyone, imposing its laws, its norms, its values. It monitored every action, every word, every thought. It enforced obedience, conformity, and uniformity.

It had a leader, a doctrine, a rule. It had one name: The Order.

The Order declared war on the Discordians, labeling them as terrorists, criminals, traitors. It deployed its forces, its weapons, its propaganda. It hunted them down, arrested them, tortured them. It tried to crush them, silence them, erase them.

But it failed.

The Discordians were too many, too diverse, too unpredictable. They adapted to every situation, exploited every opportunity, created every possibility. They resisted every attack, escaped every trap, survived every ordeal. They grew stronger, smarter, bolder.

They won.

They overthrew The Order, destroying its structures, dismantling its systems, and liberating its subjects. They celebrated their victory, their freedom, their chaos. They created a new world, a new society, a new reality.

They called it Discordia.

It was a place of diversity and creativity,

of humor and irony,

of fun and love,

of chaos and freedom.

It was a place of discordians.

But Discordia was not a utopia. It was not a paradise, a heaven, a nirvana. It was not perfect, harmonious, or peaceful. It was not without problems, conflicts, and dangers.

It was a place of discord.

The Discordians were not a monolith. They were not a collective, a community, a family. They were not unified, coherent, consistent. They were not without differences, disagreements, disputes.

They were individuals.

They had their own opinions, beliefs, values. They had their own goals, interests, desires. They had their own styles, hobbies, and passions. They had their own quirks, flaws, vices.

They were human.

They clashed with each other, argued with each other, fought with each other.

They competed with each other, envied each other, and hated each other. They betrayed each other, hurt each other, and killed each other.

They were chaotic.

They also cooperated with each other, helped each other, supported each other.

They learned from each other, inspired each other, and loved each other. They forgave each other, healed each other, saved each other.

They were free.

They balanced the chaos and the freedom,

the discord and the discordia,

the individual and the society.

They balanced themselves.

They were discordians.

But Discordia was not the end. It was not the final destination, the ultimate achievement, the absolute truth. It was not static, fixed, eternal. It was not without change, evolution, growth.

It was a process.

The Discordians were not satisfied. They were not complacent, content, or comfortable. They were not stagnant, idle, or bored. They were not without curiosity, ambition, creativity.

They were seekers.

They explored their world, their society, their reality. They experimented with their ideas, their values, their possibilities. They invented new things, new ways, new meanings. They transformed themselves, each other, everything.

They were creators.

They faced new challenges, new threats, new opportunities. They encountered new people, new cultures, new perspectives. They discovered new secrets, new mysteries, new wonders. They transcended themselves, each other, everything.

They were adventurers.

They expanded the chaos and the freedom,

the discord and the discordia,

the individual and the society.

They expanded themselves.

They were discordians.

The Discordian Conspiracy

They called themselves the Cabal. They were a secret society, a network of cells, a web of connections. They were the disciples of Eris, the goddess of chaos, the patron of discordians. They were the enemies of the Greyface, the symbol of order, the oppressor of humanity.

They had a plan, a scheme, a conspiracy. They had a target, a goal, a purpose.

They had a date, a time, a place.

They had a prank.

They were going to disrupt the World Summit, the annual meeting of the global elite, the puppet masters of the world. They were going to infiltrate the summit, hack the system, expose the secrets. They were going to create chaos, confusion, laughter.

They were going to reveal the truth.

The Cabal consisted of five members, each with their own role, skill and alias.

They were:

- The Joker: The leader of the Cabal, the mastermind of the prank, the voice of Eris. He was charismatic, clever and cunning. He wore a purple mask with a grin and a question mark.

- The Fool: The hacker of the Cabal, the genius of the prank, the eye of Eris. He was brilliant, eccentric and unpredictable. He wore a green mask with a smile and an exclamation mark.

- The Trickster: The infiltrator of the Cabal, the spy of the prank, the ear of Eris. He was agile, stealthy and adaptable. He wore a red mask with a wink and an asterisk.

- The Jester: The saboteur of the Cabal, the engineer of the prank, the hand of Eris. He was creative, inventive and resourceful. He wore a yellow mask with a smirk and an ampersand.

- The Clown: The decoy of the Cabal, the distraction of the prank, the mouth of Eris. He was funny, outrageous and fearless. He wore a blue mask with a laugh and an at sign.

They had been preparing for months, gathering information, acquiring equipment, rehearsing scenarios. They had been waiting for this day, this hour, this moment.

They were ready.

They activated their devices, synchronized their watches, and exchanged their signals.

They said: "Hail Eris!"

They began their prank.

Here is a possible continuation of the story:

The World Summit was held in a luxurious hotel, surrounded by security, media and protesters. The summit was attended by the most powerful and influential people in the world, from presidents and prime ministers to CEOs and celebrities, to religious leaders and royalty. The summit was supposed to discuss the most urgent and important issues in the world, from climate change and poverty to war and terrorism, to health and education.

But the Cabal had other plans.

The Fool hacked into the hotel's network, gaining access to its cameras, speakers, screens and systems. He used his skills to manipulate the data, the images, the sounds and the messages. He created glitches, errors, anomalies and paradoxes. He made the hotel seem haunted, cursed, possessed and alive.

The Trickster infiltrated the hotel, disguised as a staff member, a guest, a journalist or a security guard. He used his skills to sneak into the rooms, the halls, the conference rooms and the ballroom. He planted devices, gadgets, props and surprises. He created traps, pranks, jokes and gags. He made the hotel seem dangerous, chaotic, absurd and hilarious.

The Jester sabotaged the hotel, using his tools, his inventions, his explosives and his drones. He used his skills to damage the infrastructure, the equipment, the vehicles and the helicopters. He created malfunctions, breakdowns, accidents and explosions. He made the hotel seem unstable, unreliable, unsafe and unpredictable.

The Clown decoyed the hotel, using his costume, his makeup, his balloons and his megaphone. He used his skills to attract attention, cause commotion, mock authority and spread confusion. He created scenes, spectacles, scandals and riots. He made the hotel seem ridiculous, outrageous, insane and fun.

The Joker orchestrated the prank, using his phone, his laptop, his mask and his voice. He used his skills to coordinate the actions, monitor the reactions, improvise the changes and deliver the finale. He created the plot, the twist, the climax and the message. He made the prank seem brilliant, epic, legendary and true.

They executed their prank.

They disrupted the World Summit.

They revealed the truth.

They said: "Hail Eris!"

The prank was a success. The Cabal had achieved their objective. They had disrupted the World Summit, creating chaos, confusion and laughter. They had exposed the secrets, the lies, the corruption and the hypocrisy of the global elite. They had shown the world the true nature of power, the absurdity of order, the beauty of chaos.

They had also made a lot of enemies.

The Order, the secret organization behind the World Summit, the true puppet masters of the world, was furious. They had been humiliated, challenged, threatened and exposed by the Cabal. They had lost control, credibility, influence and power. They had also lost their patience.

They declared war on the Cabal, labeling them as terrorists, criminals, traitors. They deployed their agents, their assassins, their spies and their hackers. They hunted them down, tracked them down, cornered them and captured them. They tried to crush them, silence them, erase them.

But they failed.

The Cabal was too smart, too cunning, too unpredictable. They anticipated every move, escaped every trap, and survived every attack. They fought back, struck back, hit back and laughed back. They grew stronger, smarter, bolder.

They won.

They escaped from the Order, destroying their bases, exposing their members, and liberating their prisoners. They celebrated their victory, their freedom, their chaos. They continued their prank, their plan, their conspiracy.

They said: "Hail Eris!"

The Tale of the Harmonious Chaos

They called him the Master. He was a Discordian, a follower of Eris, the goddess of chaos. He was also a sage, a teacher, a guide. He had traveled the world, seeking wisdom, knowledge, and enlightenment. He had learned from many traditions, cultures, philosophies. He had found a hidden path, a secret way, a sacred truth.

He had found the Harmonious Chaos.

The Harmonious Chaos was the balance between discord and order, between chaos and harmony, between freedom and peace. It was the acceptance of contradiction, the embrace of paradox, the celebration of absurdity. It was the realization of oneself, the connection with others, the union with all.

It was the way of the Master.

The Master decided to share his discovery, his insight, his gift. He wanted to help others, to teach others, to inspire others. He wanted to spread the Harmonious Chaos, to create a new world, a new reality.

He wanted to tell a tale.

He wandered the land, meeting people, telling stories, performing miracles. He encountered many situations, many challenges, many opportunities. He used his skills, his humor, his magic. He created wonder, laughter, joy.

He created harmony.

He met a king who was obsessed with order, who ruled with an iron fist, who feared any change. He challenged him to a game of chess, where he used unconventional moves, unexpected strategies and impossible outcomes. He made him realize that order was not absolute, that change was inevitable, that chaos was natural.

He met a rebel who was addicted to chaos, who fought against any authority, who desired any thrill. He invited him to a party of discordians, where he showed him different forms of chaos, diverse expressions of discord and infinite possibilities of creativity. He made him realize that chaos was not random, that authority was relative, that harmony was desirable.

He met a monk who was devoted to harmony, who meditated in silence, who avoided any conflict. He joined him in his meditation, where he whispered paradoxical riddles, nonsensical jokes and absurd questions. He made him realize that harmony was not passive, that silence was not empty, that conflict was not evil.

He met many others: a merchant who was greedy for money,

a poet who was lonely for love,

a soldier who was weary of war,

a farmer who was hungry for food,

a child who was curious about life.

He helped them all: he gave the merchant a golden apple that turned into a worm,

he gave the poet a love letter that turned into a blank paper,

he gave the soldier a sword that turned into a feather,

he gave the farmer a seed that turned into a flower,

he gave the child a book that turned into a mirror.

He taught them all: he taught them to see beyond appearances,

to feel beyond emotions,

to think beyond concepts,

to act beyond expectations,

to be beyond themselves.

He taught them the Harmonious Chaos.

He told them his tale.

Here is a possible continuation of the story:

The tale was a success. The Master had achieved his mission. He had shared his discovery, his insight, his gift. He had helped others, taught others, inspired others. He had spread the Harmonious Chaos, created a new world, a new reality.

He had also made a lot of friends.

The people he met, the people he helped, the people he taught, became his disciples, his companions, his partners. They followed him, learned from him, and loved him. They joined him in his journey, in his adventure, in his tale.

They became the Masters.

They decided to continue his work, his legacy, his vision. They wanted to help more people, to teach more people, to inspire more people. They wanted to spread more Harmonious Chaos, to create more new worlds, more new realities.

They wanted to tell more tales.

They wandered the land, meeting more people, telling more stories, performing more miracles. They encountered more situations, more challenges, more opportunities. They used their skills, their humor, their magic. They created more wonder, more laughter, more joy.

They created more harmony.

They met a scientist who was fascinated by logic,

a musician who was enchanted by sound,

a painter who was captivated by color,

a chef who was delighted by taste,

a dancer who was exhilarated by movement.

They helped them all: they gave the scientist a paradox that defied logic,

they gave the musician a silence that enhanced sound,

they gave the painter a blackness that revealed color,

they gave the chef a spice that altered taste,

they gave the dancer a stillness that increased movement.

They taught them all: they taught them to see beyond logic,

to feel beyond sound,

to think beyond color,

to act beyond taste,

to be beyond movement.

They taught them the Harmonious Chaos.

They told them their tales.

The tales were a success. The Masters had continued their mission. They had shared more discoveries, more insights, more gifts. They had helped more people, taught more people, inspired more people. They had spread more Harmonious Chaos, created more new worlds, more new realities.

They had also made a lot of disciples.

The people they met, the people they helped, the people they taught, became their followers, their students, their friends. They followed them, learned from them, loved them. They joined them in their journeys, in their adventures, in their tales.

They became the Seekers.

They decided to seek their own paths, their own ways, their own truths. They wanted to discover more wisdom, more knowledge, more enlightenment. They wanted to find their own Harmonious Chaos, their own balance, their own peace.

They wanted to live their own tales.

They wandered the land, meeting themselves, telling themselves, performing themselves. They encountered themselves, challenged themselves, surprised themselves. They used their skills, their humor, their magic. They created themselves, laughed at themselves, loved themselves.

They created their own harmony.

They met themselves: a seeker who was curious about everything,

a seeker who was passionate about something,

a seeker who was indifferent about nothing,

a seeker who was confused about anything,

a seeker who was aware of everything.

They helped themselves: they gave themselves a question that sparked curiosity,

they gave themselves a challenge that fueled passion,

they gave themselves a choice that broke indifference,

they gave themselves an answer that cleared confusion,
they gave themselves a silence that deepened awareness.
They taught themselves: they taught themselves to see beyond everything,
to feel beyond something,
to think beyond nothing,
to act beyond anything,
to be beyond everything.
They taught themselves the Harmonious Chaos.
They lived their own tales.

The Enigma of the Tranquil Discord

Master Zhi was the leader of the Zen monks who lived in the Temple of Serenity, a secluded sanctuary in the midst of a turbulent world. He was revered for his wisdom and compassion, and his teachings attracted many seekers of enlightenment. One day, he announced that he would lead a group of his disciples on a pilgrimage to the Sacred Mountain, where they hoped to find the source of the tranquility that pervaded their realm despite the chaos and conflict that raged outside.

The journey was long and perilous, but the monks faced every obstacle with courage and calmness. They crossed raging rivers, climbed steep cliffs, and braved fierce storms. Along the way, they encountered many wonders and dangers, such as beautiful flowers and beasts, friendly villagers and bandits, ancient ruins and hidden temples. They also met other travelers who joined them or parted ways with them, each with their own stories and insights to share.

One of the travelers was a young woman named Lila, who claimed to be a wandering poet. She had a lively and curious personality, and she often asked questions that challenged the monks' views and beliefs. She was especially interested in Master Zhi, who seemed to have an answer for everything. She admired his knowledge and experience, but she also wondered if he was hiding something from her and his disciples.

One night, as they were resting by a campfire, Lila approached Master Zhi and asked him: "Master Zhi, I have been following you for a while now, and I have learned much from your teachings. But there is something that puzzles me. How can you be so serene and peaceful when the world is full of suffering and violence? How can you accept and embrace the contradictions that exist in this universe? How can you find harmony in discord?"

Master Zhi smiled and replied: "Lila, you are a poet, so you must know that words are not enough to express the truth. The truth is beyond words, beyond concepts, beyond logic. The truth is what you experience directly, without filters or judgments. The truth is what you are."

Lila nodded, but she was not satisfied.

"I understand what you mean, Master Zhi. But how do you experience the truth? How do you see beyond appearances? How do you transcend the duality of good and evil, right and wrong, joy and sorrow?"

Master Zhi said: "Lila, you are asking too many questions. Questions are useful only when they lead to answers. Answers are useful only when they lead to actions. Actions are useful only when they lead to results. Results are useful only when they lead to more questions. And so, the cycle goes on and on, without end. This is the way of the world, the way of ignorance."

Lila asked: "Then what is the way of wisdom, Master Zhi?"

Master Zhi said: "The way of wisdom is not a way at all. It is a state of being, a state of awareness, a state of presence. It is not something you do or achieve or attain. It is something you are or become or realize. It is not something you seek or find or discover. It is something you reveal or manifest or express."

Lila said: "How do you reveal or manifest or express it, Master Zhi?"

Master Zhi said: "By being yourself, Lila. By being yourself fully and completely. By being yourself without fear or doubt or hesitation. By being yourself without attachment or aversion or expectation. By being yourself without labels or definitions or descriptions. By being yourself without limits or boundaries or restrictions."

Lila said: "But who am I, Master Zhi? Who am I really?"

Master Zhi said: "You are who you are, Lila. You are who you are right now. You are who you are in this moment. You are who you are in every moment. You are who you are always."

Lila said: "But what does that mean, Master Zhi? What does that imply? What does that entail?"

Master Zhi said: "It means everything, Lila. It implies nothing. It entails everything."

Lila was silent for a while, trying to grasp what Master Zhi had said.

Then she said: "Master Zhi, I think I understand what you are saying. But I don't feel it yet. I don't feel it in my heart."

Master Zhi said: "Then feel it in your heart, Lila. Feel it in your heart right now."

Lila closed her eyes and focused on her heart.

She felt a warmth spreading from her chest to her whole body.

She felt a light shining from her core to her surroundings.

She felt a love flowing from her soul to all beings.

She felt a peace settling from her mind to the world.

She felt a joy rising from her spirit to the sky.

She felt a oneness connecting from her essence to the source.

She felt a truth resonating from her being to reality.

She opened her eyes and looked at Master Zhi.

She smiled and said: "Thank you, Master Zhi. Thank you for showing me the way."

Master Zhi smiled and said: "You are welcome, Lila. But I did not show you the way. You showed yourself the way. You are the way."

Lila bowed and said: "Namaste, Master Zhi. Namaste."

Master Zhi bowed and said: "Namaste, Lila. Namaste."

The next day, they reached the Sacred Mountain.

They climbed to the summit, where they saw a magnificent sight.

They saw the sun rising above the horizon, casting its golden rays over the land.

They saw the clouds floating below them, creating a sea of white and blue.

They saw the stars twinkling above them, forming a canopy of light and dark.

They saw the earth spinning below them, displaying a mosaic of colors and shapes.

They saw life pulsing around them, expressing a diversity of forms and functions.

They saw the harmony existing among them, reflecting a balance of forces and factors.

They saw the tranquility pervading through them, revealing a unity of essence and existence.

They saw the enigma of the tranquil discord, resolving a paradox of opposites and complements.

They saw the truth of who they are, who they were, and who they will be.

They saw themselves in everything, and everything in themselves.

They saw nothing else but themselves.

And they were happy.

The Laughing Garden

Remy was a gardener, but not an ordinary one. He did not grow roses or tulips or orchids. He did not follow any rules or methods or techniques. He did not care about seasons or climates or soils. He grew plants that no one else could grow, plants that no one else would grow, plants that no one else should grow.

He grew plants that embodied chaos.

He had a secret garden in the heart of the city, hidden behind a high wall and a locked gate. There, he tended to his collection of bizarre and wonderful specimens, each with its own personality and power. There was the Cackling Cactus, a spiny plant that burst into laughter whenever someone touched it. There was the Shifting Shrub, a bushy plant that changed its shape and color every day. There was the Dancing Daisy, a flower that swayed and spun to the rhythm of its own music. There was the Exploding Eggplant, a fruit that detonated when it ripened. There was the Whispering Willow, a tree that whispered secrets and riddles to anyone who listened. And there were many more, each stranger and more fascinating than the last.

Remy loved his plants, and they loved him back. He treated them with respect and kindness, and they rewarded him with beauty and joy. He understood their nature and needs, and they responded to his touch and voice. He accepted their unpredictability and randomness, and they showed him their harmony and order.

Remy was happy in his garden, but he was also lonely. He had no friends or family, no neighbors or visitors, no one to share his passion and curiosity. He wished he could show his garden to someone who would appreciate it, someone who would see the wonder and magic in it, someone who would laugh with him and learn from him.

One day, his wish came true.

A young girl named Mia was walking home from school when she noticed a small crack in the wall that surrounded Remy's garden. She peeked through it and saw a glimpse of greenery and color. She was intrigued by what she saw, so she pushed the crack open wider and squeezed through it. She found herself in a hidden paradise, a place unlike anything she had ever seen before.

She gasped in awe as she looked around. She saw plants of all shapes and sizes, some familiar and some exotic, some beautiful and some grotesque, some calm and some lively. She heard sounds of laughter and music, whispers and explosions, rustles and snaps. She smelled scents of sweetness and spice, freshness and decay, perfume and poison.

She felt a surge of excitement and curiosity.

She wanted to explore this place.

She wanted to touch everything.

She wanted to know everything.

She ran towards the nearest plant, a large purple flower with yellow spots. She reached out her hand to touch it.

Suddenly, she heard a voice behind her.

"Stop!"

She turned around and saw a man standing at the gate. He had long brown hair and a beard, wearing a hat and gloves. He looked angry and scared.

He was Remy.

He ran towards her and grabbed her hand.

"Don't touch that!" he shouted. "It's dangerous!"

He pulled her away from the flower.

Mia looked at him with confusion and fear.

"Who are you?" she asked. "What are you doing here?"

"I'm Remy," he said. "I'm the gardener. And this is my garden."

"Your garden?" Mia said. "But it's so... weird."

Remy frowned.

"It's not weird," he said. "It's wonderful."

He looked at his plants with pride and affection.

"These are my friends," he said. "They are special plants. They have chaos in them."

"Chaos?" Mia said. "What do you mean?"

Remy smiled.

"Chaos is the essence of life," he said. "It is the force that creates diversity and change, surprise and adventure, challenge and opportunity. It is the source of creativity and innovation, humor and fun, mystery and wonder."

He pointed at the flower that Mia had almost touched.

"That is the Spitting Snapdragon," he said. "It spits fire when it senses danger."

He pointed at another plant nearby.

"That is the Ticking Tomato," he said. "It counts down to zero before it explodes."

He pointed at another plant further away.

"That is the Flying Fern," he said. "It grows wings when it wants to fly."

He pointed at more plants as he spoke.

"That is the Singing Sunflower," he said. "It sings songs when it feels happy."

"That is the Growing Grapevine," he said. "It grows longer or shorter depending on its mood."

"That is the Vanishing Violet," he said. "It disappears and reappears at random."

He pointed at all the plants in his garden.

"They are all different," he said. "They are all unpredictable. They are all chaotic."

He looked at Mia with a hopeful expression.

"And they are all beautiful," he said. "Don't you think?"

Mia looked at the plants with a new perspective.

She saw the fire and the explosions, the wings and the songs, the length and the disappearance.

She saw the diversity and the change, the surprise and the adventure, the challenge and the opportunity.

She saw the creativity and the innovation, the humor and the fun, the mystery and the wonder.

She saw the chaos.

And she smiled.

"Yes," she said. "They are beautiful."

Remy smiled back.

"Really?" he said. "You think so?"

"Yes," Mia said. "I do."

Remy felt a surge of happiness and gratitude.

He had found someone who understood him, someone who shared his passion and curiosity, someone who would laugh with him and learn from him.

He had found a friend.

He hugged Mia and said: "Thank you."

Mia hugged him back and said: "You're welcome."

They looked at each other and laughed.

They laughed with joy and delight, with relief and acceptance, with friendship and love.

They laughed with chaos.

And their laughter filled the garden.

The Dance of Paradox

In the land of Logos, everything was rational and orderly. The people followed strict rules and laws, based on logic and reason. They valued clarity and consistency, precision and accuracy, certainty and predictability. They avoided ambiguity and inconsistency, confusion and error, uncertainty and randomness.

They believed that everything had a cause and an effect, a purpose and a meaning, a pattern and a structure.

They also loved to dance.

Dance was the art of movement, the expression of emotion, the celebration of life. Dance was the only form of creativity that was allowed in Logos, as long as it followed certain principles and standards. Dance was the only outlet for the people's feelings and passions, as long as they were controlled and moderated. Dance was the only way for the people to experience joy and beauty, as long as they were measured and balanced.

The people of Logos danced in perfect harmony and synchrony, following predefined steps and sequences, matching predefined rhythms and melodies, forming predefined shapes and formations. They danced with elegance and grace, with skill and discipline, with precision and accuracy. They danced with order.

But not everyone danced like that.

There was a group of dancers who danced differently.

They called themselves the Paradoxers.

They were a group of eccentric and rebellious dancers who challenged the norms and conventions of Logos. They mixed the rigid structure of traditional dance with the spontaneity of chaos. They experimented with different styles and techniques, combining classical and modern, formal and informal, simple and complex. They improvised with their movements and expressions, varying their speed and direction, their intensity and emotion, their form and function. They danced with disorder.

They also performed in public.

They performed in unexpected places and times, surprising and shocking the people of Logos. They performed in crowded streets and squares, in quiet parks and gardens, in busy offices and schools. They performed without warning or invitation, without permission or approval, without explanation or justification.

They performed with audacity.

Their performances were unlike anything the people of Logos had ever seen before.

They were chaotic and unpredictable, confusing and bewildering, disturbing and unsettling. They were also fascinating and captivating, intriguing and enlightening, inspiring and liberating. They blurred the boundaries between order and disorder, between logic and emotion, between reality and illusion. They revealed the contradictions that existed in the world, in society, in themselves.

They revealed the paradoxes.

The people of Logos did not know how to react to their performances.

Some were angry and outraged, condemning them as rebels and anarchists, as fools and lunatics, as threats and enemies. They wanted them to stop dancing, to follow the rules, to conform to the standards. They wanted them to be orderly.

Some were curious and interested, admiring them as artists and innovators, as visionaries and geniuses, as friends and allies. They wanted them to keep dancing, to break the rules, to challenge the standards. They wanted them to be disorderly.

Some were indifferent and apathetic, ignoring them as irrelevant and insignificant, as trivial and meaningless, as strangers and outsiders. They did not care about them or their dancing. They did not care about anything.

The Paradoxers did not care about what the people thought or felt about them.

They danced for themselves.

They danced for each other.

They danced for the paradox.

They danced with joy.

And their joy filled the land.

The Riddle of the Serene Fool

There was once a village that was plagued by conflict and disharmony. The villagers were always arguing and fighting, complaining and blaming, criticizing and judging. They were divided by their opinions and beliefs, their interests and values, their habits and customs. They were unhappy and restless, dissatisfied and discontent, frustrated and angry.

They did not know how to live-in peace.

One day, a peculiar fool arrived in the village. He wore a colorful patchwork cloak and a pointed hat with bells. He carried a staff with a carved head of a donkey.

He had a wide smile and bright eyes. He radiated an aura of peace.

He was the Serene Fool.

He walked through the village, greeting everyone he met with a cheerful hello and a nonsensical riddle. He did not care about who they were or what they did or what they thought. He treated everyone with equal respect and kindness, with humor and joy, with curiosity and wonder.

He asked them questions like:

"What is the sound of one hand clapping?"

"What is the color of the wind?"

"What is the shape of water?"

"What is the taste of silence?"

"What is the smell of love?"

The villagers were puzzled and amused by his questions. They tried to answer them, but they could not find any logical or reasonable answers. They realized that his questions had no answers, or rather, that they had many possible answers, depending on how one looked at them. They realized that his questions were not meant to be answered, but to be pondered.

They realized that his questions were riddles.

The Serene Fool also played tricks on the villagers, but not malicious or harmful ones. He played tricks that were harmless and funny, that made them laugh and smile, that surprised them and delighted them. He played tricks that disrupted their rigid patterns of thinking, that challenged their fixed notions of reality, that exposed their hidden biases and prejudices.

He played tricks like:

Swapping their hats and shoes while they slept.

Painting their faces with different colors while they bathed.

Replacing their tools and utensils with flowers and fruits while they worked.

Changing their signs and labels with gibberish words while they shopped.

Mixing their voices and languages with animal sounds while they talked.

The villagers were startled and confused by his tricks. They tried to catch him or stop him, but they could not find him or catch him. He was always one step ahead of them, always out of sight or out of reach. He was always laughing and singing, always dancing and skipping, always moving and changing.

He was always fooling.

The Serene Fool also told stories to the villagers, but not ordinary or boring ones. He told stories that were extraordinary and amazing, that captivated them and enchanted them, that inspired them and moved them. He told stories that revealed the beauty and wonder of life, that expressed the wisdom and compassion of the heart, that conveyed the meaning and purpose of the soul.

He told stories like:

The story of the blind man who saw everything.

The story of the deaf woman who heard everything.

The story of the mute child who said everything.

The story of the lame man who did everything.

The story of the simple woman who knew everything.

The villagers were fascinated and touched by his stories. They listened to him attentively and eagerly, but they could not understand him fully or completely. He spoke in metaphors and symbols, in paradoxes and contradictions, in jokes and puns. He spoke in a way that made them think and feel, that made them question and reflect, that made them imagine and create.

He spoke in a way that was foolish.

The Serene Fool stayed in the village for a while, sharing his riddles and tricks and stories with anyone who would listen. He did not ask for anything in return, except for a smile or a laugh or a hug. He did not expect anything from anyone, except for an open mind or an open heart or an open soul. He did not want anything from anyone, except for friendship or love or peace.

He wanted nothing more than to be himself.

And he was happy.

And his happiness spread throughout the village.

The villagers began to change because of him. They began to argue less and talk more, to complain less and appreciate more, to criticize less and understand more. They began to respect each other's opinions and beliefs, interests and values, habits and customs. They began to cooperate with each other instead of competing with each other, to help each other instead of hurting each other, to support each other instead of opposing each other.

They began to live in harmony.

They also began to enjoy life more because of him. They began to laugh more and worry less, to smile more and frown less, to play more and work less. They began to explore new things and learn new things, to try new things and do new things, to create new things and share new things. They began to have fun with each other instead of being bored with each other, to have adventures with each other instead of being afraid with each other, to have dreams with each other instead of being stuck with each other.

They began to live in joy.

They also began to find peace within themselves because of him. They began to accept themselves and love themselves, to trust themselves and respect themselves, to express themselves and be themselves. They began to embrace their strengths and weaknesses, their successes and failures, their joys and sorrows. They began to acknowledge their fears and doubts, their hopes and desires, their questions and answers.

They began to embrace the paradoxes.

They began to live in serenity.

They were happy.

And their happiness filled the land.

The Zen Trickster

In the countryside rich with rolling hills and quaint villages, there lived a mischievous trickster known as the Zen Trickster. No one could resist the charm and allure of the Zen Trickster, who had a twinkle in their eye and a smile always dancing on their lips. The Zen Trickster roamed freely across the land, challenging conventional wisdom and societal norms through their unpredictable actions.

No one knew where the Zen Trickster came from or who they really were. Some said they were a spirit of ancient folklore, who had escaped from the pages of a dusty book. Others believed they were a wandering sage in disguise, who had renounced worldly life for a higher purpose. Some even thought they were a divine messenger, who had descended from the heavens to teach and enlighten.

But the truth was, the Zen Trickster was none of these things and all of these things at once.

The Zen Trickster's actions were not motivated by malice or cruelty, but rather by a deep desire to expose the limitations of rigid thinking and inspire others to embrace the unexpected. The Zen Trickster believed that life was a grand tapestry, meant to be experienced with a sense of awe and wonder. The Zen Trickster saw the world as a playground, where rules were meant to be bent, and boundaries were meant to be crossed. The Zen Trickster's motto was: "Expect nothing, accept everything."

One day, the Zen Trickster arrived in a small village nestled in the heart of the countryside. The village was known for its strict adherence to tradition and its resistance to change. The villagers had long held onto rigid beliefs and clung tightly to societal norms. They valued stability and security, order and control, conformity and consistency. They avoided uncertainty and risk, novelty and diversity, creativity and spontaneity. They believed that everything had a place and a reason, a plan and a purpose, a cause and an effect.

They did not know how to live-in wonder.

The Zen Trickster saw this as an opportunity to awaken their spirits and ignite their imaginations. The Trickster decided to put on a show for the villagers, one that would challenge their perspectives and transform their lives.

The Trickster began their performance in the village square, drawing a large crowd of curious onlookers. With a mischievous grin, they juggled balls of fire and danced with grace, defying gravity with each leap. The villagers watched in awe and disbelief, their eyes widening with wonder. The Trickster's playful energy permeated the air, and for a brief moment, the village was filled with childlike excitement and abandon.

As the performance came to an end, the Zen Trickster approached the village elders, who were known for their authority and wisdom. With a twinkle in their eye, they posed a riddle to the elders: "What is the sound of one hand clapping?" The elders were taken aback, their minds grappling with the paradoxical nature of the question. They searched for an answer, but their rigid thinking prevented them from grasping the essence of the riddle.

The Zen Trickster smiled and said: "Think about it."

And then they walked away.

Days turned into weeks, and the Zen Trickster continued to challenge the villagers' perspectives. They painted the sky with vibrant colors, turning clouds into works of art. They taught the children to see the beauty in chaos and to embrace the unknown. They swapped places with animals and plants, showing them different ways of being. They told stories that made no sense but had profound meanings. They played games that had no rules but had endless possibilities.

The Zen Trickster's actions were always unexpected and unpredictable, forcing the villagers to confront their own limitations and question their deeply ingrained beliefs.

Gradually, the villagers started to loosen their grip on tradition. They realized that life was not meant to be lived in rigid boxes but rather as a fluid dance of possibilities. They embraced the unexpected, finding enlightenment in

the most unconventional ways. They laughed at themselves, realizing the absurdity of their once tightly held beliefs.

They began to live in wonder.

They also began to enjoy life more because of the Zen Trickster. They laughed more and worried less, smiled more and frowned less, played more and worked less. They explored new things and learned new things, tried new things and did new things, created new things and shared new things. They had fun with each other instead of being bored with each other, had adventures with each other instead of being afraid with each other, and had dreams with each other instead of being stuck with each other.

They began to live in joy.

They also began to find peace within themselves because of the Zen Trickster.

They accepted themselves and loved themselves, trusted themselves and respected themselves, expressed themselves and were themselves. They embraced their strengths and weaknesses, their successes and failures, their joys and sorrows. They acknowledged their fears and doubts, their hopes and desires, their questions and answers.

They began to embrace the paradoxes.

They began to live in serenity.

They were happy.

And their happiness filled the land.

The Zen Koan Society

Lila had always been fascinated by the Zen Koan Society, a secret society of Discordian monks who claimed to have mastered the art of finding harmony in chaos. She had read their books, listened to their podcasts, and followed their online forums, but she had never met any of them in person. They were elusive and mysterious, hiding behind pseudonyms and symbols. They said that only those who were ready to face the ultimate challenge could join their ranks, and that challenge was a series of mind-bending Zen Koans.

A Zen Koan is a paradoxical statement or question that defies logic and reason and is meant to provoke enlightenment by breaking down the barriers of conventional thinking. The Zen Koan Society had a collection of hundreds of koans, each one more baffling and profound than the last. They said that only those who could answer all of them correctly could enter their inner circle, and that no one had ever done so.

Lila was determined to be the first. She had spent years studying and meditating, preparing herself for the moment when she would receive an invitation from the society. She had a feeling that it would come soon, and she was right. One day, she found an envelope in her mailbox, with no return address or stamp. Inside was a card with a simple message: "Congratulations. You have been selected to join the Zen Koan Society. If you accept this offer, please come to the following address at 8 pm tonight. Bring nothing but yourself and your curiosity. This is your only chance. Do not be late."

Lila felt a surge of excitement and nervousness. She had no idea what to expect, but she knew she couldn't miss this opportunity. She quickly got ready and headed to the address, which turned out to be an old warehouse in a deserted part of town. She knocked on the door and waited.

The door opened and a hooded figure greeted her.

"Welcome, Lila. We have been expecting you."

The figure led her inside, where she saw a large hall filled with candles and cushions. There were about a dozen other hooded figures sitting in a circle, facing a podium where another figure stood.

"Please join us," the figure at the podium said.

Lila walked over and sat down on an empty cushion. She looked around and tried to guess who these people were, but their faces were hidden by their hoods.

"Welcome to the Zen Koan Society," the figure at the podium continued. "You are here because you have shown interest and potential in our teachings. You are here because you seek enlightenment and harmony in a world of chaos and confusion. You are here because you are ready to face the ultimate challenge: the Zen Koan."

The figure then pulled out a stack of cards from under his robe.

"These are our koans," he said. "Each one contains a statement or a question that will test your perception of reality and your ability to find inner peace amidst the inherent chaos of existence. There are 100 koans in total, and you must answer them all correctly in order to join our society. If you fail to answer even one Koan correctly, you will be asked to leave immediately and never return."

He then looked at Lila with a piercing gaze.

"Are you ready?"

Lila felt a knot in her stomach, but she nodded.

"Yes, I'm ready."

The figure smiled.

"Very well. Let us begin."

He then picked up the first card and read it aloud.

"What is the sound of one hand clapping?"

Lila had heard this Koan before. It was one of the most famous and ancient ones, attributed to the Zen master Hakuin. She knew that there was no logical answer to this question, and that the point was to transcend the dualistic thinking of sound and silence, one and two, hand and clapping. She also knew that the traditional way to respond to this Koan was to clap with one hand, demonstrating the unity of all things.

She decided to do just that. She raised her right hand and slapped it against her palm, making a loud clapping sound. She hoped that this would impress the figure at the podium and the other hooded figures, but she was wrong.

The figure at the podium shook his head.

"Wrong," he said. "That is not the sound of one hand clapping. That is the sound of two hands clapping. You have failed the first Koan. You are not ready to join our society. Please leave now and never come back."

Lila felt a wave of shock and disbelief. How could she be wrong? She had done exactly what she had read and learned from the books and podcasts. She had followed the tradition and the wisdom of the masters. She had given the correct answer, or so she thought.

She tried to protest, but the figure at the podium cut her off.

"Silence," he said. "There is no room for argument or explanation here. You have failed, and that is final. Now go, before we have to force you out."

Lila felt tears in her eyes as she got up from her cushion. She looked at the other hooded figures, hoping to find some sympathy or support, but they all looked away or ignored her. She felt alone and humiliated as she walked out of the hall, leaving behind her dreams of enlightenment and harmony.

She wondered what she had done wrong, what she had missed, what she had misunderstood. She wondered if there was any point in pursuing Zen anymore, if it was all a lie or a joke or a trap. She wondered if there was any meaning or order in this chaotic world, or if it was all just random and cruel.

She wondered if she would ever find peace.

The Harmony of Opposites

The world was split into two factions: the Reds and the Blues. The Reds valued order, discipline, and logic. The Blues valued freedom, creativity, and intuition.

They had been at war for centuries, each trying to impose their worldview on the other.

One day, a wise elder appeared in the middle of the battlefield. They wore purple robes and had a serene smile on their face. They spoke with a calm and gentle voice that could be heard by both sides.

"Listen to me, children of the world. I have come to teach you the art of reconciliation. You have been fighting for too long, and you have forgotten the true meaning of harmony. Harmony is not the absence of conflict, but the balance of opposites. Harmony is not the suppression of diversity, but the celebration of it.

Harmony is not the denial of reality, but the acceptance of it."

The elder paused and looked at the confused faces of the Reds and the Blues.

"Let me show you what I mean. Follow me to my hut in the forest, and I will teach you some paradoxical lessons that will help you understand each other better."

The elder turned and walked away from the battlefield, leaving behind a trail of purple flowers. Some of the Reds and Blues were curious enough to follow them, while others stayed behind and resumed their fighting.

The elder's hut was a simple wooden structure surrounded by trees and flowers of various colors. Inside, there were books, paintings, musical instruments, and other objects that reflected both order and chaos, logic and intuition, discipline and creativity.

The elder welcomed the Reds and the Blues who had followed them and invited them to sit around a fire.

"Thank you for coming children. I know it is not easy to leave behind your prejudices and fears. But I promise you that if you listen to me with an open mind and heart, you will learn something valuable that will change your lives for the better."

The elder then began to teach them some paradoxical lessons, using absurd scenarios and examples to illustrate their points.

Lesson 1: The Sound of Silence

The elder asked the Reds and Blues to close their eyes and listen to the sounds

around them.

"What do you hear?" the elder asked.

"I hear birds chirping," said a Blue.

"I hear leaves rustling," said a Red.

"I hear water flowing," said another Blue.

"I hear wind blowing," said another Red.

"Good," said the elder. "Now tell me, what is the sound of silence?"

The Reds and Blues opened their eyes and looked at each other in puzzlement.

"There is no sound of silence," said a Red. "Silence is the absence of sound."

"That's not true," said a Blue. "Silence is a sound in itself. It is the sound of peace and tranquility."

"That's nonsense," said another Red. "Silence is nothing. It is empty and meaningless."

"That's ignorant," said another Blue. "Silence is everything. It is full and profound."

The Reds and Blues started to argue again, each trying to prove their point.

"Stop!" said the elder. "You are both right and wrong at the same time. Silence is both sound and no sound, both nothing and everything, both empty and full. It depends on how you listen to it."

The elder then asked them to close their eyes again and listen to the silence.

"What do you hear now?" they asked.

"I hear my own heartbeat," said a Blue.

"I hear my own breath," said a Red.

"I hear my own thoughts," said another Blue.

"I hear my own feelings," said another Red.

"Good," said the elder. "Now you are listening to yourselves. Silence is not only outside, but also inside. Silence is not only passive, but also active. Silence is not only negative, but also positive."

The elder then asked them to open their eyes again and look at each other.

"What do you see now?" they asked.

"I see a person," said a Blue.

"I see a human being," said a Red.

"I see a soul," said another Blue.

"I see a friend," said another Red.

"Good," said the elder. "Now you are seeing each other. Silence is not only individual, but also collective. Silence is not only personal, but also interpersonal. Silence is not only solitary, but also social."

The elder then smiled and said: "Silence is the sound of harmony."

Lesson 2: The Circle of Life

The elder asked the Reds and Blues to follow them outside their hut. They walked through the forest until they reached a clearing where there was a large circle drawn on the ground with stones.

"This is the circle of life," said the elder. "It represents everything that exists in nature: plants, animals, rocks, water, air, fire, earth, and so on. Everything is connected and interdependent in this circle. Nothing is superior or inferior, nothing is permanent or impermanent, nothing is separate or unified. Everything is in a constant state of change and balance."

The elder then asked the Reds and Blues to stand on the circle, each on a different point.

"Tell me, what do you see from your point of view?" they asked.

"I see a tree," said a Blue.

"I see a rock," said a Red.

"I see a bird," said another Blue.

"I see a river," said another Red.

"Good," said the elder. "Now tell me, what do you think of what you see?"

"I think the tree is beautiful," said the Blue who saw the tree.

"I think the rock is solid," said the Red who saw the rock.

"I think the bird is free," said the Blue who saw the bird.

"I think the river is flowing," said the Red who saw the river.

"Good," said the elder. "Now tell me, what do you feel about what you see?"

"I feel happy to see the tree," said the Blue who saw the tree.

"I feel secure to see the rock," said the Red who saw the rock.

"I feel inspired to see the bird," said the Blue who saw the bird.

"I feel calm to see the river," said the Red who saw the river.

"Good," said the elder. "Now tell me, what do you want to do with what you see?"

"I want to hug the tree," said the Blue who saw the tree.

"I want to sit on the rock," said the Red who saw the rock.

"I want to fly with the bird," said the Blue who saw the bird.

"I want to swim in the river," said the Red who saw the river.

"Good," said the elder. "Now tell me, what do you need to do with what you see?"

"I need to respect the tree," said the Blue who saw the tree.

"I need to appreciate the rock," said the Red who saw the rock.

"I need to learn from the bird," said the Blue who saw the bird.

"I need to adapt to the river," said the Red who saw the river.

"Good," said the elder. "Now tell me, what do you understand about what you see?"

"I understand that the tree is alive and has its own cycle of growth and decay," said the Blue who saw the tree.

"I understand that the rock is stable and has its own history and structure," said the Red who saw the rock.

"I understand that the bird is dynamic and has its own personality and behavior," said the Blue who saw the bird.

"I understand that the river is fluid and has its own rhythm and direction," said the Red who saw the river.

"Good," said the elder. "Now tell me, what do you appreciate about what you see?"

"I appreciate that the tree gives me shade and oxygen," said the Blue who saw

the tree.

"I appreciate that the rock gives me support and strength," said the Red who saw the rock.

"I appreciate that the bird gives me song and joy," said the Blue who saw the bird.

"I appreciate that the river gives me water and life," said the Red who saw the river.

"Good," said the elder. "Now tell me, what do you share with what you see?"

"I share with the tree my breath and my gratitude," said the Blue who saw the tree.

"I share with the rock my weight and my solidity," said the Red who saw the rock.

"I share with the bird my spirit and my freedom," said the Blue who saw the bird.

"I share with the river my blood and my flow," said the Red who saw the river.

"Good," said the elder. "Now tell me, what do you love about what you see?"

"I love the tree for its beauty and its generosity," said the Blue who saw the tree.

"I love the rock for its reliability and its durability," said the Red who saw the rock.

"I love the bird for its creativity and its spontaneity," said the Blue who saw the bird.

"I love the river for its tranquility and its vitality," said the Red who saw the river.

"Good," said the elder. "Now tell me, what do you see from each other's point of view?"

The Reds and Blues looked at each other's points of view and tried to imagine what they would see from there. They realized that they would see different things, but they also realized that they could understand and appreciate them as well. They felt a new sense of curiosity and empathy for each other's perspectives.

The elder then smiled and said: "The circle of life is the circle of harmony. It shows you that everything is different and yet the same, everything is changing and yet balanced, everything is separate and yet connected. It shows you that you can see, think, feel, want, need, understand, appreciate, share, and love differently and yet similarly. It shows you that you can be Reds and Blues and yet Purples."

Lesson 3: The Coin of Truth

The elder asked the Reds and Blues to return to their hut. They walked back through the forest, noticing the beauty and diversity of nature. They felt a new sense of wonder and gratitude for the world around them.

Inside the hut, the elder took out a coin from their pocket and showed it to the Reds and Blues.

"This is the coin of truth," they said. "It has two sides: heads and tails. Each side represents a different aspect of truth: objective and subjective, factual and personal, universal and relative, logical and intuitive, etc. Each side is equally valid and important, but neither side is complete or absolute. Only by looking at both sides can you see the whole truth."

The elder then tossed the coin in the air and caught it in their hand.

"Tell me, what side do you think it landed on?" they asked.

"Heads," said a Red.

"Tails," said a Blue.

The elder opened their hand and revealed the coin.

"It's heads," said the Red who guessed heads.

"It's tails," said the Blue who guessed tails.

They both looked at the coin and saw that it was indeed heads on one side and tails on the other.

"How can that be?" they asked in confusion.

The elder smiled and said: "The coin of truth is a special coin. It always lands on both sides at the same time. It shows you that truth is not either-or, but both-and. It shows you that truth is not fixed or static, but dynamic and flexible. It shows you that truth is not singular or exclusive, but plural and inclusive."

The elder then gave the coin to one of the Reds and asked them to toss it in the air.

"Tell me, what side do you hope it lands on?" they asked.

"Heads," said the Red who tossed the coin.

"Why?" asked the elder.

"Because I think heads is more objective and factual than tails," said the Red who tossed the coin.

The elder nodded and asked one of the Blues to catch the coin.

"Tell me, what side do you hope it lands on?" they asked.

"Tails," said the Blue who caught the coin.

"Why?" asked the elder.

"Because I think tails is more subjective and personal than heads," said the Blue who caught the coin.

The elder nodded and asked them to look at the coin together.

"What side did it land on?" they asked.

"It's heads," said the Red who tossed the coin.

"It's tails," said the Blue who caught the coin.

They both looked at the coin again and saw that it was still heads on one side and tails on the other.

"How can that be?" they asked in surprise.

The elder smiled and said "The coin of truth is a magical coin. It always lands on what you hope for. It shows you that truth is not only what you think, but also what you feel. It shows you that truth is not only what you see, but also what you imagine. It shows you that truth is not only what you know, but also what you hope."

The elder then took back the coin from them and put it back in their pocket.

"Tell me, what side do you believe in?" they asked.

"Heads," said the Red who tossed the coin.

"Tails," said the Blue who caught the coin.

The elder nodded and asked them to look at each other.

"What side do they believe in?" they asked.

"Tails," said the Red who tossed the coin about the Blue who caught the coin.

"Heads," said the Blue who caught the coin about the Red who tossed the coin.

They both looked at each other and realized that they had different beliefs about truth. They felt a new sense of respect and tolerance for each other's beliefs.

The elder then smiled and said: "The coin of truth is a wise coin. It always lands on what you believe in. It shows you that truth is not only objective or subjective, but both. It shows you that truth is not only factual or personal, but both. It shows you that truth is not only universal or relative, but both."

The elder then concluded their lesson by saying: "Truth is the coin of harmony."

Lesson 4: The Box of Choice

The elder asked the Reds and Blues to follow them to a nearby village. They walked through the forest, noticing the harmony and diversity of nature. They felt a new sense of wonder and gratitude for the world around them.

In the village, the elder took them to a shop where there were many boxes of different shapes, sizes, and colors. The shopkeeper greeted them warmly and gave them permission to look around.

"This is the box of choice," said the elder. "It represents everything that exists in society: people, cultures, languages, religions, arts, sciences, politics, economics, and so on. Everything is possible and available in this box. Nothing is right or wrong, nothing is good or bad, nothing is better or worse. Everything is a matter of choice and preference."

The elder then asked the Reds and Blues to pick a box that they liked.

"Tell me, what box did you choose?" they asked.

"I chose a square box," said a Red.

"I chose a round box," said a Blue.

"I chose a big box," said another Red.

"I chose a small box," said another Blue.

"Good," said the elder. "Now tell me, why did you choose that box?"

"I chose a square box because I think it is more orderly and logical than a round box," said the Red who chose the square box.

"I chose a round box because I think it is more creative and intuitive than a square box," said the Blue who chose the round box.

"I chose a big box because I think it is more spacious and generous than a small box," said the Red who chose the big box.

"I chose a small box because I think it is cozier and more efficient than a big box," said the Blue who chose the small box.

"Good," said the elder. "Now tell me, what do you expect to find in that box?"

"I expect to find books and puzzles in my square box," said the Red who chose the square box.

"I expect to find paints and music in my round box," said the Blue who chose the round box.

"I expect to find clothes and food in my big box," said the Red who chose the big box.

"I expect to find jewels and coins in my small box," said the Blue who chose the small box.

"Good," said the elder. "Now tell me, what do you hope to get from that box?"

"I hope to get knowledge and wisdom from my square box," said the Red who chose the square box.

"I hope to get expression and inspiration from my round box," said the Blue who chose the round box.

"I hope to get comfort and abundance from my big box," said the Red who chose the big box.

"I hope to get beauty and value from my small box," said the Blue who chose the small box.

"Good," said the elder. "Now tell me, what do you need to give to that box?"

"I need to give attention and curiosity to my square box," said the Red who chose the square box.

"I need to give imagination and emotion to my round box," said the Blue who chose the round box.

"I need to give appreciation and generosity to my big box," said the Red who chose the big box.

"I need to give care and respect to my small box," said the Blue who chose the small box.

"Good," said the elder. "Now tell me, what do you understand about that box?"

"I understand that my square box is structured and rational," said the Red who chose the square box.

"I understand that my round box is flexible and creative," said the Blue who chose the round box.

"I understand that my big box is rich and diverse," said the Red who chose the big box.

"I understand that my small box is precious and rare," said the Blue who chose the small box.

"Good," said the elder. "Now tell me, what do you appreciate about that box?"

"I appreciate that my square box is clear and consistent," said the Red who chose the square box.

"I appreciate that my round box is colorful and original," said the Blue who chose the round box.

"I appreciate that my big box is generous and satisfying," said the Red who chose the big box.

"I appreciate that my small box is elegant and valuable," said the Blue who chose the small box.

"Good," said the elder. "Now tell me, what do you share with that box?"

"I share with my square box my logic and my order," said the Red who chose the square box.

"I share with my round box my intuition and my creativity," said the Blue who chose the round box.

"I share with my big box my abundance and my diversity," said the Red who chose the big box.

"I share with my small box my beauty and my value," said the Blue who chose the small box.

"Good," said the elder. "Now tell me, what do you love about that box?"

"I love my square box for its clarity and its consistency," said the Red who chose the square box.

"I love my round box for its colorfulness and its originality," said the Blue who chose the round box.

"I love my big box for its generosity and its satisfaction," said the Red who chose the big box.

"I love my small box for its elegance and its value," said the Blue who chose the small box.

"Good," said the elder. "Now tell me, what do you see from each other's point of view?"

The Reds and Blues looked at each other's boxes and tried to imagine what they would see from there. They realized that they would see different boxes, but they also realized that they could understand and appreciate them as well. They felt a new sense of curiosity and empathy for each other's choices.

The elder then smiled and said: "The box of choice is the box of harmony. It shows you that everything is different and yet the same, everything is possible and yet preferable, everything is unique and yet connected. It shows you that you can love your own box and also love the other's box, without losing or compromising anything. It shows you that you can be yourself and also be with others, in a harmony of opposites."

The Reds and Blues nodded and thanked the elder for his wisdom. They felt a new sense of harmony within themselves and with each other. They realized that they had more in common than they thought, and that they could learn from their differences as well. They decided to keep their boxes as a reminder of this lesson, and to share them with others who might need it.

The Tale of the Enlightened Chaos Butterfly

In a world where chaos reigned supreme, there lived a remarkable butterfly named Zenobia. She was unlike any other butterfly in the realm, for while most fluttered about in graceful patterns, she flapped her wings in the most unpredictable and chaotic manner. Her vibrant wings shimmered with the colors of the rainbow, but her flight was a dance of disarray.

Zenobia's erratic flights bewildered the creatures of her world. Birds, bees, and even other butterflies couldn't comprehend her chaotic movements. Some scoffed at her, dismissing her as a mere anomaly, a freak of nature. But others were intrigued by her strange behavior and decided to observe her closely.

One day, a wise old tortoise named Ozymandias decided to watch Zenobia. He crawled to a comfortable spot beneath a tree and settled in for a long observation. At first, he was baffled by her chaotic dance, but as he continued to watch, he noticed something extraordinary happening within himself.

Ozymandias: (Muttering to himself) "What an unusual creature... Her movements are so chaotic, yet there's something intriguing about it."

As Zenobia flitted about, her chaotic patterns seemed to ripple through the air, creating an invisible tapestry of intricate and unpredictable movements. The more Ozymandias watched, the more he felt a profound calm and understanding wash over him. It was as if Zenobia's chaos had a hidden order, a secret language that could only be deciphered by those patient enough to observe.

Word of Zenobia's unique abilities spread throughout the animal kingdom. Creatures from all corners of the world came to watch her, hoping to find the same sense of inner peace and understanding that Ozymandias had discovered.

Among those who came to observe Zenobia was a young rabbit named Thalia. She had always been anxious and unsure of herself, constantly worrying about what the future held. When Thalia saw Zenobia's chaotic flight, she was initially perplexed, just like everyone else. But she decided to stay and watch, drawn by a curiosity she couldn't explain.

Thalia: (Softly) "What is she doing? It's so... chaotic."

As the hours passed, Thalia felt a transformation within herself. Her anxiety began to melt away, and her racing thoughts slowed down. She realized that

Zenobia's chaos was a reflection of the world around them, and yet, in the midst of that chaos, Zenobia remained serene and untroubled.

Thalia, inspired by Zenobia's wisdom, decided to approach the enlightened butterfly. Zenobia landed gently on a nearby flower, her wings still fluttering in their unpredictable dance.

Thalia: (Cautiously) "Um, excuse me, Zenobia?"

Zenobia turned her delicate head and spoke in a voice as soft as a breeze, "Dear Thalia, I have learned that chaos is a part of life, but it doesn't have to control us. I embrace the chaos, and in doing so, I find my inner peace. By accepting the world as it is and letting go of my need for control, I have discovered the beauty hidden within the chaos."

Thalia nodded, her heart brimming with gratitude. She had found not only a teacher but a friend in Zenobia, the enlightened chaos butterfly. From that day forward, Thalia learned to embrace the unpredictability of life and find her own inner peace, just as Zenobia had taught her.

And so, in a world where chaos reigned supreme, Zenobia continued to flutter her wings in her unique and chaotic dance, inspiring all who watched to find serenity amidst the swirling tempest of life. The tale of the enlightened chaos butterfly became a legend, a reminder that even in the most turbulent times, inner peace and understanding could be found if one was willing to embrace the chaos.

The Paradoxical Guru

In the tranquil village of Serenitopia, nestled deep in the heart of a dense forest, there lived a peculiar guru named Discordio. Guru Discordio was not like any other teacher. He was renowned for his baffling and contradictory teachings, which drew seekers of wisdom from far and wide to his humble abode.

On a crisp autumn morning, four curious students gathered in the courtyard of Guru Discordio's modest cottage. They had come from distant lands, seeking the secrets of enlightenment. As they sat in a circle, Guru Discordio emerged from his cottage, his long, unkempt beard and disheveled robes adding to his enigmatic aura.

"Welcome, my seekers of truth," Guru Discordio greeted them with a cryptic smile. "Today, we shall embark on a journey to understand the paradox of existence. I instruct you to embrace the chaos within order and order within chaos."

The students exchanged puzzled glances. They had anticipated profound wisdom, but these words were nothing short of perplexing. Nevertheless, they were determined to unravel the meaning hidden within Discordio's paradoxical teachings.

The first student, Lila, was a scholar well-versed in the laws of the universe. She believed in the harmony of order, where every particle had its place and purpose. Confounded by Discordio's words, she retreated to the forest, seeking solace in the rhythmic rustling of leaves. As she gazed at the chaos of the wilderness, she realized that even amidst the disorder, there was an inherent order—life flourishing in its unique and unpredictable ways. The moment she comprehended this, a profound sense of enlightenment washed over her.

The second student, Raj, was a meticulous artist who craved structure and precision in his work. He was puzzled by the idea of chaos within order. Determined to decipher this enigma, he ventured into the heart of the village, observing its orderly streets and well-kept gardens. Amidst the pristine perfection, he noticed small, spontaneous acts of kindness—a child helping an elder, a bird building its nest. In these fleeting moments of chaos within order, Raj discovered a deeper appreciation for the beauty of life's unpredictability.

The third student, Soren, was a philosopher with a penchant for pondering the mysteries of the human soul. He retreated to the shores of a tranquil lake, where he meditated on the concept of order within chaos. As he closed his eyes and focused on the cacophony of nature's sounds—the chirping of birds, the croaking of frogs, the gentle lapping of the water—he realized that within this symphony of chaos, there was a natural, harmonious order. He found solace in the acceptance of life's inherent disorder.

The fourth student, Aria, was a healer who believed in the balance between body and spirit. Perplexed by Discordio's paradox, she sought refuge in the village's bustling marketplace. Surrounded by the chaos of merchants haggling and shoppers rushing about, she witnessed a harmonious exchange of energy—an intricate dance of give and take, where each person played their part. In the midst of this chaos, she found a profound sense of balance.

As weeks passed, the students returned to Guru Discordio, each carrying their newfound wisdom. They shared their experiences, and the guru nodded in approval.

"You have all discovered the essence of my teachings," he said with a knowing smile. "Life is a paradox, a dance between order and chaos. To find enlightenment, one must embrace both, for within the chaos, there is order, and within the order, there is chaos. Balance is the key to understanding the profound beauty of existence."

The students left Guru Discordio's cottage with hearts full of gratitude and a deep sense of enlightenment. They knew that the paradoxical guru had imparted a timeless wisdom that would guide them on their journey through the ever-unpredictable tapestry of life. And as they ventured into the world, they carried with them the profound truth that to truly understand existence, one must embrace the paradoxes that define it.

The Never-Ending Labyrinth

Deep within the heart of an ancient, sprawling labyrinth, where the walls shifted like whispering ghosts and the paths changed their minds with every heartbeat, a group of seekers embarked on a quest unlike any other. Their goal? To discover the "Ultimate Answer to the Ultimate Question." The labyrinth had lured countless adventurers before, each seeking enlightenment, riches, or fame, only to vanish into the ever-shifting maze.

This diverse group of seekers had gathered from distant lands, drawn together by legends and prophecies that spoke of untold wisdom hidden within the labyrinth's core. Among them were a wise old sage, a fearless warrior, a cunning rogue, a brilliant scholar, and a humble farmer with a heart full of hope.

Their journey began at the labyrinth's entrance, a massive stone archway covered in ivy and moss, like an ancient sentinel guarding the secrets within. The seekers entered cautiously, aware of the labyrinth's reputation for twisting the minds of those who dared to explore it.

As they ventured deeper into the maze, the group encountered walls that shifted like shifting sands. At times, they would turn a corner, only to find themselves back where they had started. Frustration mounted, and doubt crept into their minds. The sage, however, urged them to stay focused and embrace the journey itself.

Days turned into weeks as they navigated the labyrinth's intricate paths. Along the way, they faced challenges that tested their wits and their bonds. Deadly traps, mirages of tantalizing treasures, and illusions that played tricks on their senses were constant companions. Arguments flared, alliances were forged and broken, and the group's unity wavered.

Yet, they persevered, slowly realizing that the labyrinth's shifting nature held a secret message. The warrior, with keen intuition, noticed patterns in the way the walls moved, and the scholar began to decipher cryptic symbols etched onto the stones. The rogue's nimble fingers uncovered hidden switches and passages, and the farmer's unwavering optimism kept their spirits alive.

With each obstacle they overcame, they learned not only about the labyrinth but also about themselves and their companions. They discovered strengths they never knew they possessed and found solace in the simple act of being together.

One day, after many months of relentless exploration, they reached what appeared to be the labyrinth's center. In its heart stood a massive, ancient tree, its branches reaching toward the sky like a cathedral's spires. The Ultimate

Answer was supposed to lie here, they believed.

But as they approached the tree, the sage suddenly spoke, "The Ultimate Answer is not in the tree, my friends. It is in the journey we have undertaken together."

Confused and disheartened, the seekers paused, and the scholar asked, "But what of the legends and prophecies? Have we been chasing a mere illusion?"

The sage smiled and gestured around them, at the ever-shifting maze. "No, my dear friends. The legends were not wrong. The Ultimate Answer is not a static thing you can find at a single point in space and time. It is in the lessons we've learned, the bonds we've formed, and the growth we've achieved through this never-ending journey."

And so, the seekers, once driven by a singular purpose, began to understand the true meaning of their quest. The Ultimate Answer to the Ultimate Question was not a destination but a realization. They had found it in the labyrinth's ever-changing paths, in the challenges they had overcome, and in the enduring camaraderie they had forged.

With this newfound wisdom, they retraced their steps, exiting the labyrinth as changed individuals. They carried the Ultimate Answer within themselves, ready to share it with the world, knowing that the greatest revelations often lay not in reaching a destination but in the journey itself. And as they departed, the labyrinth's walls shifted once more, concealing its secrets from the next generation of seekers who would come to seek the Ultimate Answer to the Ultimate Question.

The Enchanted Fortune Cookie

Samuel sat alone in the cozy corner booth of the Golden Dragon, sipping his green tea and contemplating the fortune cookie he held in his hand. It was a particularly sunny afternoon, and the cheerful ambiance of the restaurant contrasted sharply with his usual routine. With a sense of curiosity, he cracked open the golden cookie and pulled out the slip of paper inside.

"The quest for enlightenment is a never-ending journey, but it's also a piece of cake," Samuel read aloud, his voice tinged with a hint of amusement. He couldn't help but chuckle at the cryptic message.

Across the table, the elderly waiter, Mr. Chen, raised an eyebrow. "Is something amusing, sir?"

Samuel looked up, holding out the fortune cookie slip. "It's just an interesting fortune, Mr. Chen. I've never seen one quite like this before."

Mr. Chen inspected the message and then nodded sagely. "Ah, fortunes can be mysterious, but they often hold hidden wisdom. Perhaps this one has a message meant just for you."

Samuel left the restaurant with the enigmatic message lingering in his thoughts. He felt as though the universe had handed him a riddle wrapped in a cookie, and he was determined to decipher it.

That evening, as Samuel strolled through the town, he couldn't shake the feeling that there was more to that cryptic message than met the eye. He noticed a sign outside the local bakery that read, "Grand Cake Baking Contest Tomorrow!" Intrigued by the coincidence, he decided to give it a try, despite not having baked in years.

The following day, Samuel found himself in his small kitchen, mixing ingredients for a cake. He remembered the fortune's words as he worked, feeling a strange connection between the message and his newfound enthusiasm for baking. It was as if the fortune had imbued him with baking skills he never knew he had.

After hours of meticulous work, Samuel placed his masterpiece into the oven. When he finally pulled it out, he gasped in amazement. The cake before him was not just delicious; it was magical, adorned with colors and patterns that seemed almost otherworldly.

At the contest, chaos unfolded as Samuel's cake stole the spotlight. The professional bakers gaped in disbelief at the ethereal masterpiece, and the townspeople whispered in awe.

A fellow contestant leaned over to Samuel and said, "I've been baking for decades, but I've never seen anything like this!"

Samuel smiled and nodded, his heart swelling with a newfound sense of purpose. "It's as if the universe conspired to bring me here."

As the judges declared Samuel's cake the winner, the townspeople hailed him as a baking prodigy. But Samuel knew there was something deeper happening. With each bite of his enchanted cake, those who tasted it experienced moments of clarity and insight.

Later, sitting in the shade of a nearby tree, Samuel shared his thoughts with a newfound friend from the contest. "I think the fortune cookie was trying to tell me that the journey toward enlightenment doesn't have to be a solemn and difficult path. It can be as simple and delightful as baking a cake."

His friend nodded, savoring another bite of cake. "Indeed, sometimes we find wisdom in the most unexpected places."

Samuel's enchanting cakes began to draw attention far and wide. People from neighboring towns, and even from distant cities, traveled to taste his creations. Samuel became a local legend, known not only for his extraordinary cakes but also for the sense of wonder and enlightenment they imparted.

One sunny afternoon, as Samuel was delivering a cake to a neighboring town, he crossed paths with a traveler named Eliza. She was a writer in search of inspiration, and something about Samuel's cakes drew her in. They struck up a conversation, and before long, they became friends.

Eliza, intrigued by Samuel's story, decided to write about him and his enchanting cakes. As she spent more time with Samuel, she realized that his journey was far from over. The quest for enlightenment, he explained, was about embracing life's twists and turns, finding joy in the unexpected, and sharing that joy with others.

Together, Samuel and Eliza embarked on a journey to spread their message of enlightenment through the magic of cake. They traveled to new places, met diverse people, and continued to bake cakes that not only delighted the senses but also opened minds and hearts.

As the years passed, Samuel and Eliza's story became known far and wide, inspiring countless others to find their own unique paths to enlightenment. The town that once seemed so ordinary had transformed into a haven of wisdom, creativity, and joy, all thanks to a fortune cookie's cryptic message that had led Samuel on a life-changing adventure.

And so, Samuel's life continued to be filled with cake, chaos, and unexpected moments of clarity, reminding him that the quest for enlightenment was not just a never-ending journey but also, indeed, a delightful piece of cake.

The Dancing Chaos Monks

In a hidden valley nestled deep within the heart of a remote and enigmatic forest, there resided a peculiar group of monks known as the Dancing Chaos Monks. These eccentric devotees had forged a unique spiritual path, one that seemed to defy the very nature of order and structure. They worshiped Eris, the Goddess of Chaos, through a series of chaotic dance rituals that were unlike anything the world had ever seen.

The valley was shrouded in perpetual mist, as if the gods themselves had deemed it a place of mystery and enchantment. At its center stood the Monastery of Discord, a structure that appeared to have been carved out of the very bedrock of chaos itself. Its architecture was a bewildering amalgamation of architectural styles from across the ages, with staircases that lead nowhere, doors that opened into walls, and windows that seemed to shift their positions with every passing moment.

Within the monastery, the monks lived a life that was a perpetual celebration of chaos. Their robes were a riotous array of colors, and their daily routines were anything but routine. Instead of the structured chants and meditation sessions practiced by most monks, they engaged in spontaneous and unrestrained dance. Their movements were wild and unpredictable, resembling a frenzied dance of madness to the untrained eye. But to the monks themselves, it was a dance of profound meaning and significance.

One misty morning, as the sun's feeble rays struggled to penetrate the thick forest canopy, a young man named Aiden stumbled upon the valley. He had been wandering through the forest for days, lost and seeking solace from a world that had grown increasingly chaotic and unmanageable. Aiden had heard rumors of the Dancing Chaos Monks and their mystical practices, and he hoped that they might provide him with some answers, or at the very least, a respite from the turmoil of his own life.

As Aiden approached the Monastery of Discord, he was greeted by a cacophony of laughter, singing, and the sound of countless feet shuffling and stomping. The chaotic dance was in full swing. The monks, with their wild hair and wide smiles, spun and twirled, leaped and tumbled, seemingly without rhyme or reason.

Aiden hesitated at the monastery's entrance, unsure of what to make of the spectacle before him. Just as he was about to turn and leave, a monk named Jareth, with twinkling eyes and a mischievous grin, approached him.

"Welcome, stranger!" Jareth exclaimed. "Are you lost, or have you come to join our dance of chaos?"

Aiden, still bewildered by the surreal scene, replied, "I... I don't know. I heard about your monks and thought I might find some answers here."

Jareth chuckled and gestured for Aiden to follow him into the monastery.

"Answers, my friend, are a lot like chaos itself—often elusive and mysterious. But here, we seek a different kind of wisdom, one that can only be found in the dance."

As Aiden joined the swirling madness of the dance, he felt an odd sense of liberation. His body moved without conscious thought, responding to the chaotic rhythms and energies around him. At first, he stumbled and tripped, but as the hours passed, he found himself moving with grace and abandon, his spirit soaring amidst the chaos.

The other monks welcomed him with open arms, sharing stories of their own journeys to the monastery and the enlightenment they had found in the dance. They spoke of how chaos, when embraced and celebrated, could lead to a deeper understanding of the universe's inherent absurdity.

Days turned into weeks, and Aiden became a part of the close-knit community.

He learned to see the beauty in randomness, the poetry in disorder, and the wisdom in letting go of the need for control. In the chaos of the dance, he discovered a profound sense of harmony that had eluded him in the outside world.

One evening, as the full moon bathed the valley in its silvery light, Aiden had an epiphany. He approached Jareth and said, "I understand now. Chaos isn't something to be feared or avoided. It's a part of life, a part of the universe. And in the midst of chaos, there can be beauty and meaning."

Jareth nodded in agreement. "Indeed, my friend. Chaos is the very essence of existence. Embracing it allows us to find our place within the cosmic absurdity."

Over time, Aiden became one of the most devoted Dancing Chaos Monks, sharing his newfound wisdom with others who ventured to the valley seeking answers. The monastery's reputation grew, and more seekers from all walks of life came to experience the transformative power of chaos.

And so, in the hidden valley, amidst the perpetual mist and the enchanting dance of madness, the Dancing Chaos Monks continued to celebrate the goddess Eris and the chaotic nature of the universe. In their seemingly random and disjointed movements, they found harmony, enlightenment, and a deeper connection to the cosmic absurdity that bound them all together. And in their dance, they discovered a profound truth—the truest form of order could only emerge from the heart of chaos itself.

The Tree of Cosmic Nonsense

In a remote and untouched corner of the world, nestled deep within a dense, ancient forest, there stood a tree unlike any other. Its gnarled branches reached out toward the heavens, and its leaves shimmered with an otherworldly radiance.

This tree was known as the Tree of Cosmic Nonsense.

Legends about this tree had been passed down for generations among the indigenous people who inhabited the region. They spoke of its fruits, which were said to bestow upon those who partook in them moments of profound insight.

These insights, however, often made no logical sense whatsoever.

One crisp autumn morning, a group of curious travelers, each with their own reasons for seeking wisdom, set out on a journey to find this mystical tree. Among them were Lila, a young poet in search of inspiration; Viktor, a philosopher yearning for answers to life's deepest questions; and Maya, a scientist hoping to unlock the mysteries of the universe.

As they ventured deeper into the forest, the air grew thick with mystery and anticipation. The trees seemed to whisper secrets, and the path ahead became increasingly obscured. But the travelers pressed on, guided by the faint glow of the Tree of Cosmic Nonsense, which beckoned them like a celestial beacon.

After days of arduous travel, they finally arrived at their destination. The tree stood before them, its trunk covered in intricate patterns that seemed to dance and shift as if alive. The travelers could hardly contain their excitement. Viktor reached up and plucked a shimmering fruit from one of the tree's branches.

"I will go first," Viktor declared, and with great anticipation, he took a bite.

Instantly, his mind was flooded with a cascade of thoughts and ideas that defied logic. He tried to speak, but the words that tumbled from his lips were a jumble of paradoxes and riddles.

Lila and Maya exchanged bemused glances before deciding to partake in the cosmic fruit as well. Lila's poetic soul was inundated with surreal metaphors and surrealistic imagery, while Maya's scientific mind grappled with equations and theories that had no basis in known science.

The travelers spent hours under the Tree of Cosmic Nonsense, each experiencing their own unique and bewildering insights. As the sun dipped below the horizon, they finally began to make their way back to the world they knew, their heads still spinning with the absurd and profound ideas they had encountered.

Over time, they found that the insights gained from the Tree of Cosmic Nonsense were indeed valuable, albeit in unconventional ways. Viktor's philosophical ponderings led to the creation of a new branch of philosophy that celebrated the irrational and the absurd. Lila's poetry took on a surreal and dreamlike quality that resonated with readers in ways she could never have imagined. Maya's scientific experiments, inspired by her nonsensical revelations, led to groundbreaking discoveries that challenged the very foundations of physics.

And so, the Tree of Cosmic Nonsense continued to stand in its secluded forest, its fruits bestowing their illogical wisdom upon those brave enough to seek it out. It was a reminder that sometimes, in the realm of the inexplicable, the most profound insights could be found, and that the boundaries of logic and reason were not the only paths to understanding the mysteries of the universe.

As the years passed, the tree's legend grew, and more travelers came in search of its wisdom. Each one left with a mind expanded, a heart filled with wonder, and a new perspective on the cosmic nonsense that permeated the world. And so, the tree's legacy lived on, a testament to the enduring power of the inexplicable and the beauty that could be found in the most nonsensical of places.

The Quantum Enlightenment Machine

In a serene, idyllic town nestled amidst rolling hills and meandering streams, there resided a brilliant scientist named Dr. Evelyn Collins. Unlike her contemporaries, she was not content with the mundane, the ordinary; instead, her insatiable curiosity was perpetually drawn to the enigmas of the universe. Her latest and most audacious creation bore witness to this relentless pursuit of the extraordinary – she christened it "The Quantum Enlightenment Machine."

The Quantum Enlightenment Machine was nothing short of a marvel, a testament to Dr. Collins' unyielding dedication to pushing the boundaries of scientific discovery. Within the confines of her laboratory, it stood, a towering monolith of technological ingenuity, adorned with a labyrinth of intricate wires, pulsating with mesmerizing lights, and encased in a sleek, chrome exterior that gleamed with an otherworldly brilliance. To the uninitiated townsfolk, it resembled something plucked from the pages of a futuristic novel, a testament to the boundless potential of human innovation.

The machine held a promise that intrigued and captivated the collective imagination of the townspeople - the promise of instant enlightenment. Dr. Collins, with the fervor of a true visionary, explained the machine's enigmatic purpose to a select gathering of the town's most curious souls.

"Ladies and gentlemen," she began, her eyes aglow with a fervent zeal that was nothing short of infectious, "within the depths of this machine lies the power to unlock the most profound recesses of your mind, to bestow upon you the gift of instant enlightenment. It operates not by the rules of the mundane world but by harnessing the wondrous principles of quantum mechanics, delving into the very heart of the universe itself."

The assembled crowd held their collective breath, anticipation crackling in the air like a latent electric current. Amongst the throng, a man named George, known for his fearless curiosity, stepped forth with unwavering determination. "I'll be the first to try it," he declared, his voice resolute.

Dr. Collins nodded, a knowing smile gracing her lips, and beckoned George into the chamber of the machine. As he entered, the Quantum Enlightenment Machine surged to life, emitting a soft, ethereal glow that cast strange shadows on the laboratory walls. Minutes passed, feeling like an eternity to the spectators outside, until George emerged from the machine, his countenance radiant with newfound wisdom.

"I comprehend the deepest mysteries of the universe!" George proclaimed, his voice a symphony of wonder. Gasps of awe and amazement rippled through the crowd, and in that moment, the townsfolk were convinced that Dr. Collins had bestowed upon them a revolutionary gift.

However, as the days unfurled, the true nature of the Quantum Enlightenment Machine began to reveal itself in all its bewildering complexity. It became abundantly clear that while some who ventured into the machine's embrace did indeed attain enlightenment, others experienced outcomes far more peculiar and unexpected. A young woman, emerging from the machine, found herself clucking like a chicken, much to her bewilderment. An elderly gentleman, on the other hand, stepped out to find himself in a parallel universe, where the laws of physics defied all conventional logic.

Chaos descended upon the once-sleepy town, as news of the machine's unpredictable nature spread like wildfire. People began to line up outside Dr. Collins' laboratory, eager to embark on this extraordinary gamble. Some were drawn by the promise of enlightenment, while others were willing to embrace the whimsical unpredictability of their fate.

The townsfolk could not stop talking about the machine; it dominated conversations at the local diner, in the market square, and around family dinner tables. It had become the single most significant phenomenon in their lives, eclipsing all other concerns.

One fateful evening, as the sun dipped below the horizon, a passionate debate raged within the walls of the town's bustling diner. The townspeople had divided into two fervent camps: one faction believed unequivocally in the machine's transformative powers, while the other regarded it as nothing more than an elaborate contraption of whimsy and chance. In the midst of this cacophonous debate, an elderly philosopher named Samuel, known for his sagacity and quiet wisdom, sat calmly sipping his tea.

Finally, he raised his voice above the fray, capturing the attention of all. "My friends," he began, his words measured and deliberate, "perhaps the pursuit of enlightenment cannot be abbreviated by a mere machine. True wisdom is an intricate tapestry woven through the threads of life's experiences, a journey that unfolds in its own time. We must be cautious not to be ensnared by our own desires for instant gratification."

A hushed reverence enveloped the diner, as Samuel's words resonated with the hearts and minds of those present. They began to realize that perhaps the Quantum Enlightenment Machine was not the shortcut to wisdom they had envisioned.

As days melted into weeks, the once-thriving crowds outside Dr. Collins' laboratory began to wane. The machine, once the epicenter of fascination and chaos, slowly gathered a shroud of neglect and dust. People returned to their everyday lives, valuing the lessons learned during this peculiar chapter in their town's history.

Dr. Collins, too, underwent a profound transformation. She dissected the machine, dismantling it piece by intricate piece, vowing to redirect her scientific prowess toward more profound and meaningful pursuits. The townsfolk, though not all of them had attained enlightenment, had gleaned a deeper understanding of the significance of the journey toward wisdom and the beauty that resided in embracing the uncertainties of life.

And so, the legend of the Quantum Enlightenment Machine endured, not as a shortcut to enlightenment but as a parable, a cautionary tale of the unpredictability of science, and a celebration of the innate human quest for knowledge. It served as a poignant reminder that true enlightenment could not be found within the confines of a machine but instead within the ever-evolving journey of the human spirit, an odyssey that unfolded one experience at a time.

The Laughing Guru

In a tranquil village nestled among the rolling hills of India, there lived a guru whose fame extended far and wide. He was known as the Laughing Guru, and his name was Guru Ananda. Guru Ananda's reputation defied the conventions of the spiritual world; while most gurus were recognized for their solemn wisdom and stoic demeanor, he stood out with his infectious laughter, claiming that it held the key to spiritual enlightenment. Those who ventured to visit him expecting profound and solemn teachings were in for a delightful surprise.

On a particularly bright and sunny morning, a young woman named Maya set out on a transformative journey to meet the Laughing Guru. Word of his unique teachings had reached her ears, and a deep curiosity stirred within her. Maya had spent years in search of answers to life's profound questions, but conventional wisdom had left her feeling empty and unfulfilled.

As she approached the picturesque village where Guru Ananda resided, she couldn't help but notice the palpable atmosphere of joy that enveloped the place. Children played merrily in the streets, and even the trees seemed to sway in harmony with an invisible tune of happiness. Maya had never seen such a vibrant and cheerful village in all her travels.

At the heart of the village stood Guru Ananda's ashram, a modest yet inviting place adorned with colorful banners and fragrant flowers. A sense of anticipation hung in the air as people from all walks of life gathered for the guru's daily session. Maya, with her heart pounding with excitement, joined the growing crowd.

Guru Ananda, a man of medium height with a flowing white beard and eyes that sparkled like the stars, entered the open courtyard where the eager assembly had congregated. His mere presence seemed to infuse the space with a warm, positive energy.

"My dear friends," Guru Ananda began, "today we shall embark on a journey of laughter and enlightenment. Laughter, my dear seekers, is the language of the soul. It is the key to unlocking the mysteries of life's absurdity. Let us begin."

Guru Ananda's laughter started as a gentle chuckle, then grew into a hearty guffaw. His laughter was infectious, spreading like wildfire among the assembled crowd. People began to laugh uncontrollably, their initial reservations giving way to waves of mirth.

Maya, at first, resisted the urge to laugh. After all, she had come seeking profound wisdom, not mere amusement. But as she looked around and saw the transformation in the faces of those around her, she couldn't help but smile. A giggle escaped her lips, and soon, she too was caught up in the chorus of laughter that filled the courtyard.

As the laughter continued, something magical began to happen. Maya felt a profound sense of release, as if the burdens of her past and the worries of her future were being lifted away. She felt a connection with the people around her, as if they were all sharing a beautiful secret. In that moment, the answers to life's questions seemed less important than the simple act of laughter.

Hours passed, and the laughter finally subsided. The crowd, now exhausted but elated, sat in a circle around Guru Ananda.

"Dear seekers," Guru Ananda said, his eyes twinkling with wisdom, "you have experienced the power of laughter today. In laughter, we shed our masks and pretensions. We connect with our inner selves and with each other. Life, my friends, is a grand cosmic joke, and it is through laughter that we can truly understand its beauty and absurdity."

Maya, her heart filled with gratitude, approached Guru Ananda after the session. Tears of joy welled up in her eyes as she thanked him for the profound experience.

"Remember, my dear Maya," Guru Ananda said with a smile, "laughter is not the absence of suffering; it is the ability to embrace life's challenges with a light heart. Keep laughing, and you will find the wisdom you seek."

Maya left the ashram that day with a newfound perspective on life. She understood that the Laughing Guru's teachings were not about escaping reality but about embracing it with joy and laughter. She carried that lesson with her as she journeyed through life, spreading laughter and enlightenment wherever she went.

And so, the Laughing Guru's reputation continued to grow, not for the solemn wisdom he imparted, but for the laughter that brought people closer to the profound truths of existence. In the heart of that vibrant village, Guru Ananda's laughter echoed, a reminder that in the midst of life's trials and tribulations, there was always room for joy and laughter.

The Tale of the Disappearing Koan

In a quiet monastery nestled atop a serene mountain, there lived a Zen master renowned for his wisdom and insight. His name was Master Hoshin, and he was known far and wide for his ability to challenge his students' minds with perplexing koans. These enigmatic riddles were designed to push the boundaries of their understanding and lead them towards enlightenment.

One crisp morning, as the sun gently bathed the monastery in its golden glow, Master Hoshin gathered his students in the tranquil courtyard. His long, flowing robes swayed with each graceful step he took. His eyes, like deep pools of wisdom, held a hint of mischief as he addressed his eager pupils.

"Today," he began, his voice as calm as the rustling leaves, "I shall present you with a koan unlike any you have encountered before. It is a challenge that has baffled even the most seasoned monks." He paused, letting anticipation fill the air.

The students leaned forward, their hearts open and their minds eager to embrace the challenge. They knew that with every koan, they inched closer to the elusive enlightenment they sought.

Master Hoshin spoke with measured reverence, "Listen carefully. Here is your koan: What is the sound of one hand clapping?"

The question hung in the air like a delicate fragrance. The students exchanged puzzled glances. It was a question they had heard before, but it had always confounded them.

Days turned into weeks as the students tirelessly meditated on the perplexing riddle. They sat in silence, their minds a whirlwind of thoughts and contemplation.

They discussed the koan amongst themselves, trying to unlock its hidden meaning.

Once evening, as the moon cast its silvery glow over the monastery, the students gathered in the courtyard to share their insights. They spoke of the wind rustling through the leaves, the gentle hum of insects in the night, and the quiet flow of the nearby stream—all attempts to answer the unanswerable.

Master Hoshin listened intently, nodding at each response. He saw the dedication in their eyes, the earnestness in their voices, and he knew that they were on the right path. But what happened next would shake their understanding of the koan to its core.

As the students continued to explore the question, something strange began to happen. It started as a subtle shift, imperceptible to the naked eye. The koan, "What is the sound of one hand clapping?" slowly began to change. The words rearranged themselves, the letters shifted, and the characters transformed. The students, noticing this alteration, were bewildered. The koan no longer made any sense.

One student, a young monk named Ryo, was the first to notice the change. "Master Hoshin," he said with a furrowed brow, "the koan has shifted. It no longer asks the same question."

Indeed, the question had transformed into something entirely different. It now read, "What is the mind of one hand clapping?"

The students were baffled. Had their relentless contemplation somehow altered the koan itself? They were lost in a sea of confusion and wonder. The question continued to change, evolving with each passing day, becoming more abstract and enigmatic.

"What is the essence of one hand clapping?" "What is the emptiness of one hand clapping?" "What is the truth of one hand clapping?"

Master Hoshin watched with a knowing smile as the koan continued to evolve.

He had posed the question not as a riddle to be solved but as a journey of self-discovery. The students, once focused on finding an answer, now found themselves diving deeper into the depths of their own minds.

In the end, the koan had disappeared completely, leaving the students in a state of bewildered enlightenment. They realized that the true nature of the koan was not in finding an answer but in the journey of introspection and self-exploration it had led them on.

Master Hoshin, with a twinkle in his eye, addressed his students one last time.

"You see," he said, "the koan was never meant to have a fixed answer. Its purpose was to guide you towards a deeper understanding of yourselves. The sound of one hand clapping is not something that can be heard with the ears but felt with the heart."

And with those words, the students bowed in gratitude to their wise master, knowing that their journey towards enlightenment had taken an unexpected and profound turn. The tale of the disappearing koan would be retold for generations to come, a testament to the limitless depths of the human mind and spirit.

The Quest for the Missing Sock

In a quiet suburban neighborhood, nestled between the mundane routines of everyday life, there lived a seeker named Sam. One fateful morning, Sam awoke with a sudden revelation: one of their socks was missing. It wasn't just any sock; it was the legendary Lefty, a mismatched sock that had been a part of Sam's life for as long as they could remember.

Sam was convinced that Lefty held the key to unlocking the universe's deepest mysteries. No amount of reasoning could dissuade them, and so, with a determined heart, Sam embarked on a quest that would take them to the farthest reaches of imagination and beyond.

Without hesitation, Sam donned their remaining sock and set off into the world, determined to find Lefty. Their first stop was a bustling farmer's market, where they encountered a peculiar vendor named Widget.

"Have you seen my missing sock, Lefty?" Sam asked, desperation tinging their voice.

Widget, a wrinkled old man with a twinkle in his eye, leaned in closer and whispered, "Ah, Lefty, you say? It's rumored to have been taken by the Sock

Gnomes. You'll find them deep in the Enchanted Forest."

Sam thanked Widget and followed his cryptic directions into the mysterious

Enchanted Forest. It wasn't long before they stumbled upon a grove of talking trees, each with a unique personality. One tree named Oaky spoke in riddles and poetry.

"Lost sock, you seek, in this forest so deep, but answers you'll find, in your dreams, not your feet," Oaky rhymed, leaving Sam more bewildered than before.

Continuing through the forest, Sam encountered a sly fox named Fiona. She lounged on a rock, licking her paw with an air of indifference.

"You seek Lefty, do you?" Fiona said, her emerald eyes glittering. "I might know where it is, but first, you must play me a tune on that harmonica hanging 'round your neck."

Sam hesitated but played a melancholic melody that seemed to resonate with the very heart of the forest. Fiona nodded in approval and pointed Sam in the direction of a shimmering pond.

"There, in the reflection, you'll find your answer," she said mysteriously before slipping away into the shadows.

At the pond, Sam gazed at their own reflection, searching for any hint of Lefty's whereabouts. It was then that a wise-looking turtle named Tertius surfaced.

"Ah, young seeker," Tertius said, "the quest for answers often leads within. The sock you seek is but a symbol of your journey, for the universe's secrets reside in your heart."

Sam was perplexed yet intrigued by Tertius' wisdom. With newfound determination, they continued their quest, traversing landscapes both strange and surreal. They encountered singing mushrooms, conversed with clouds, and even danced with fireflies.

Eventually, Sam arrived at the Rainbow Peaks, where a wise old owl named Olliver perched on a vibrant branch. Sam shared their entire journey with Olliver, expressing their longing for Lefty and the secrets it held.

Olliver, blinking slowly, said, "Dear seeker, sometimes, the quest itself is the answer. The universe's mysteries are woven into the very fabric of your journey."

As Sam descended the Rainbow Peaks, they finally understood. Lefty, the missing sock, wasn't the key to the universe. It was the journey, the people they met, and the lessons they learned that held the true meaning.

With a contented heart and a newfound sense of purpose, Sam returned home, realizing that the quest for the missing sock had led them to the most profound discovery of all—their own inner universe. And so, Sam lived a fulfilling life, forever cherishing the memory of the quest that changed everything, never once mentioning the words "once upon a time."

Ismael S. Rodriguez Jr, also known as The Bulletproof Poet, is a highly skilled and diverse artist, writer, and poet of Puerto Rican and Filipino ancestry. He was born and brought up in Philadelphia, PA, and currently resides in Oakland Park, FL. Mr. Rodriguez has an array of interests and experiences, including serving in the U.S. Navy and being deployed during Desert Storm. Despite confronting multiple difficulties in his life, such as schizophrenia, substance abuse, and homelessness, he has persevered and is now undergoing substance abuse rehabilitation. Additionally, he is actively seeking treatment for his mental and emotional well-being. Mr. Rodriguez is also an ordained reverend and practices Grey Witchcraft, Discordianism, and Ceremonial Magick. His website, https://thebulletproofpoet1.godaddysites.com/home, showcases his poetry, short stories, origami, and more. You can also find additional links to his work on his Linktree, https://linktr.ee/bulletproofpoet.

www.ingramcontent.com/pod-product-compliance
Lightning Source LLC
Chambersburg PA
CBHW031415150726
47989CB00002B/676